THE THREE FATES

Translated from the French by Mark Polizzotti

A NEW DIRECTIONS BOOK

Originally published by Editions Christian Bourgois, Paris, France, in 1997 as
    Les trois Parques. Published by arrangement with Editions Christian Bourgois.

New Directions gratefully acknowledges the support of a Hemingway Grant
    and a CNL award.
*Cet ouvrage, publié dans le cadre d'un programme d'aide à la publication, béné-
    ficie du soutien du Ministère des Affaires étrangères et du Service Culturel de
    l'Ambassade de France aux Etats-Unis.* This work, published as part of a pro-
    gram of aid for publication, received support from the French Ministry
    of Foreign Affairs and the Cultural Services of the French Embassy in the
    United States.
This work is published with support from the French Ministry of Culture/
    Centre national du livre.

Manufactured in the United States of America
Published simultaneously in Canada by Penguin Books Canada, Ltd.
New Directions Books are printed on acid-free paper.
First published as a New Directions Paperbook (NDP1179) in 2010

Library of Congress Cataloging-in-Publication Data
Lê, Linda.
[Trois Parques. English]
The three fates / Linda Lê ; translated from the French by Mark Polizzotti.
p. cm.
ISBN 978-0-8112-1610-4 (pbk. : alk. paper)
1. Vietnamese—France—Fiction. I. Polizzotti, Mark. II. Title.
PQ2672.E1113T7613 2010
843'.914—dc22

                              2009053829

10 9 8 7 6 5 4 3 2 1

New Directions Books are published for James Laughlin
by New Directions Publishing Corporation
80 Eighth Avenue, New York 10011

Come at dawn, brave friend, come at dawn.

We recognized one another, erased one another, *friend whom I cherished above all others.*

I, present at my birth. I, at my death.

And I wandered through the deserts of this world and even in death will I search for you, you, who have been the place of love.

—Alejandra Pizarnik, *Extraction of the Madness Stone*

HE WAS TIRED, BROKEN. HE AWAITED THE END, SITTING in his small blue house like King Lear in his hovel, stripped clean and abandoned by his daughters. Leave King Lear alone, I'd told my cousins, but they wouldn't listen. They had abandoned King Lear to his small blue house. They had neglected him for twenty years, and now they were conspiring like a pair of Cordelias to bestow one last joy on the old monarch. He hadn't asked for it. This final joy—actually the first, belatedly granted—would, I'd predicted, turn his world upside-down. I trusted the itch in my stump, which had started up the minute my cousins mentioned granting the forgotten old man his one last joy. My stump can always foretell disaster, I insisted, raising my voice a notch. But since they'd decided long ago that my insistence on warding off any good thing was just a byproduct of my infirmity, my cousins usually let me prattle on like some bird of ill omen—prattlings that only the younger one sometimes tried to curtail. Look, Southpaw, we've had it up to here with your premonitions, she spat that particular day. We were at my older cousin's home, her spanking new house. The kitchen, recently delivered in modular components and assembled with care, gleamed brightly, reflecting as if in a mirror the elder's round belly and the younger's long legs. If King Lear had been there, he too could have admired the gleaming kitchen, its owner's round belly, the nymph's long legs. My cousins, seized by impatience since early August, were bent on summoning King Lear as soon as possible. The best thing, the older one said, would be to take advantage of a long absence by the master of the household, her husband, the Zurich expatriate, the nutsandbolts manufacturer who every Wednesday evening attended Buddhist meditations, who every Sunday went on retreat at a Tibetan prayer center a few miles from the spanking new house, and who, every time the Dalai Lama visited France, shut down his small business, having earned admission to the sovereign's innermost circle. That year, the great Lama had announced a European tour for the fall, and well before summer the seeker of wisdom had prepared his backpack, hiking boots, dictionary, *Book of the Dead,* singing bowl, the whole kit and caboodle. The enlightened one would be ferrying the Dalai Lama across Europe and my cousins would play cicerones for King Lear, who could stay in the spanking new house, in the future child's nursery, freshly wallpapered with huge pink elephants. A white crib and white chest of drawers were scheduled for delivery, between which would be enough space for the English sofa bed that my cousin had bought on impulse and temporarily installed in a corner of the dining room. A tingling sensation swarmed over my left wrist, intensifying as my cousins' plans gelled around the large gleaming table. I had remained standing by the sink. The tap reflected red apples arranged in a pyramid in a bowl. With my right hand I plucked one of the apples, which I rolled between the table and my stump to ease the itch. Southpaw, that's gross! my younger cousin whined. She uncrossed her long legs, stood, and snared an apple of her own, which she polished on her faded cutoffs before crunching. Meanwhile my older cousin had pulled from the drawer under the sink a notepad that she balanced on her swollen belly. Mumbling, she scribbled a column of figures. I replaced the red apple at the top of the pyramid. The tingling had not subsided. I rubbed my stump against the waistband of my pants and the scratchiness of the fabric soothed the itch. My younger cousin had moved toward the French doors leading to the garden; she stood on tiptoe and tossed away the apple core, which landed in the cherry tree next door. King Lear's vacation is going to cost a mint, Potbelly said, disheartened by the prospect of picking up the entire tab, since Long Legs earned peanuts at the telemarketing firm—and even then, only when said legs deigned to show up and slide into the little cubicle equipped with phone, through which my younger cousin surveyed the preferences of the hoi polloi, yawning until her jaw nearly dropped off: *tea or coffee? toast or cereal? canned or frozen? briefs or boxers?* Question from telemarketer to owner of spanking new house: *Under what conditions would you welcome, for a finite length of time, an elderly person into your home? Only if that person were directly related to you. Only if you have neglected that person for a great many years. Only if that person were to express his gratitude in advance.* There's the rub. There was no discernible trace of thankfulness in King Lear's replies to my older cousin's invitation. As proof, she tried to produce the last letter received, which she had pressed in one of her cookbooks and now couldn't find. Damn that letter. Tucked away somewhere. Surely at the page for rösti, which she'd learned to cook in case the Zurich expatriate got homesick. The letter was not at the page for rösti. So then it must have arrived on lamb kidney day—a foul mess, seared into everyone's memory; the whole thing had to be thrown out. The letter remained missing. *The Great Book of Salads* was shaken, in vain. It fell to the floor, followed by *Art of the Fondue.* My cousin dropped into her chair, let out a sigh of exasperation, and caressed her belly to calm the little prince, whom all the ballyhoo had disturbed. The child of wisdom, the future heir to the gleaming kitchen, was already kicking up a fuss. My cousin rested a hand on her womb to placate him. Things won't be so peaceful when he starts talking, she said. It was a real puzzler, what language the little prince should speak. French, of course—that was a given. It was lingua franca in the spanking new house. But in their seed of paradise, Father dreamed of implanting some germs of German, to which Mother, not to be left behind, would marry unwonted gametes, specks of Vietnamese blown in by the winds of memory. It was the language of King Lear, after all, and thus our childhood patois, which I claimed to have forgotten—as did my younger cousin, who'd never understood a blessed word of what King Lear was jabbering about. No point looking for the letter, then, because it would have to be translated, and my cousin was sick of playing interpreter (for the depilatoried long legs, which would have avoided the sun like the plague had they remained in the tropics, and for Southpaw, who had severed the umbilical cord and now pulled a horrified grimace at the sound of that barbaric yawp, like some patient who'd come *this close* and dreaded contamination by flying spittle). Someone had to guard the temple. And, since at the mere mention of their native backwater Southpaw started humming dreary anthems, while the long legs crossed and uncrossed out of sheer boredom, Potbelly, lumbering over the finish line that her competitors had left clear for her, carried off the Trophy of Memory and the First Prize for Virtue. All that remained, to seal her pious reputation, was to procure the neglected old man one last joy, make him leave his squalor, cross the oceans, and come applaud this display and disposition of domestic virtues—the little family, the gleaming kitchen, and the child's nursery, which the old man could inaugurate and inhabit for three weeks, maybe a month, but no longer. Just long enough to let him tour the domain, fill his lungs with contentment, and finger some opulence—before they shipped him back to the tropics and his small blue house, where he could relive his ascent to Heaven while waiting for death. My younger cousin had sat at the table again, her long legs stretched out on a chair pushed toward me. She'd only have to show them to King Lear, her nude, brown, jittery, thoroughbred legs—legs that would allow her, in the steeplechase of this world, to leap tall obstacles and vault over life, or what strands of life she saw in this

6

gleaming kitchen, strands that ended in an invisible slipknot just waiting to strangle the mistress of the household. Who, absorbed in her daily evaluation of the weight ballasting her midsection, did not feel the threat of the yoke, but instead congratulated herself on having finished with her pre-conjugal state and the tedium of her own company. The nutsandbolts manufacturer and his kitbag of Tibetan wisdom had shown up just in time. In a matter of months, the wilted flower, stimulated by the new tropism of good sense, had been revived, blossoming for all to see. (Only Southpaw found something to criticize: she stood there glowering at the round belly, scratching her stump and ruminating on her horrible thoughts like some shriveled brown plant that reeked of death, sending the household gods scattering and visiting ruin on the new home.) My cousin was determined to defend her hearth and her *little family* against the mute and sinister imprecations of Ms. Southpaw, who had always enjoyed calling down disaster with all her might. (There she was, like a port-wine stain on a virgin forehead, an oozing pustule on smooth skin; there she was with her dark clothes, missing hand, messily chopped hair, her two black marble eyes that gave you the creeps, her little orphan's voice with its endless refrain of *He'snotcrazy! He'snotcrazy!* and that repulsive habit of rubbing her stump on anything within reach in the new house—tablecloths, napkins, cushions, bedspreads, and now apples.) All in all, my cousin viewed her younger sister's frivolity with a less censorious eye. Junior had but one care in the world: her long legs. She showed them off a bit too freely, sometimes tossing in her alluring navel as a bonus; and so she was welcome in the spanking new house only on those days when Hardware Man was preparing for his meditations. For while my older cousin did not feel the threat of the yoke, she clearly sensed the danger posed to her household deities by Southpaw and Long Legs, Pythia and the nymph, both bent on shattering the happiness of the *future little family,* one by marking every object in the new house with her baneful stamp, the other by parading her fillyesque body before the seeker of wisdom, whose glazed eyes then threw off sparks, promptly extinguished by the conjugated assault of Germanic circumspection and Tibetan restraint. My older cousin had gotten up to leaf through her cookbooks again. She absolutely had to read us King Lear's letter with its show of indifference. As if he didn't feel the itch to enjoy some creature comforts, to turn his back on Saigon and leave behind his ruined palace facing the new white colonnaded villas that were sprouting up like saprophytes. Saigon, to hear King Lear tell it, was infested with saprophytes. In the sky rose gigantic concrete saprophytes, which drew from the earth two-footed saprophytes, a new species that was spawned by international air travel and festered in the city after the rainy season—so King Lear had written. Apparently, one could allow oneself to say anything nowadays. My older cousin still remembered the years when she'd imagined that a greeting to Uncle Ho or a tribute to the liberators of Saigon, at the close of every letter home, would protect the little blue house and its occupant from Communist wrath. Saigon now had too much on its hands with the saprophytes to watch over the outpourings of escapees or the scribblings of little old men who had never amounted to anything, still sitting in their ruined palaces, watching the world spin along without them and waiting for death. For twenty years King Lear had been watching the world spin without him. For twenty years he had not budged from the blue house where my cousins had left him. From his ruined palace, he had witnessed the exodus of the runaways, the year when Saigon had changed hands. And now he saw the return of the saprophytes, and King Lear snickered by his window. The ruined palace, in the midst of the clean white villas, retreated increasingly into itself, like an aged eunuch in a bedful of virgins. King Lear was in decline. He walked haltingly. His joints ached in the rainy season. When he'd had enough of sitting still and listening to his bones creak and whine, he went out to tend his flowers in the garden, the small enclosure in front of his ruined palace. Seen from afar, it looked more like a tomb—not very fresh but well manicured, King Lear had written to my older cousin, taking the opportunity to request some seeds and bulbs. He wanted all kinds of flowers for his palace, rare and wild, bright and dull, scentless and fragrant, sunflowers and queens of the night. She only had to send the seeds: he'd take care of making them grow. Even crossbreed a little. It had come over him suddenly. A whim. A good ten years ago. At the time, the saprophytes weren't yet sprouting in Saigon. All around the blue house, the old palaces were still standing, but the city was dying of hunger. King Lear, too. Hunger must have eaten away at his brain, said my older cousin. He had only one thing on his mind, growing flowers. Instead of asking for care packages to help him survive, King Lear had them send tulip bulbs.

Dredging up all those memories gave my cousin an appetite, and in mid-afternoon she was overcome with a sudden urge to wolf down the leftovers of last night's dinner: squid Provençal, immediately yanked from the fridge, reheated over low flame, and thoroughly chewed by the starveling, who stared straight ahead without a word, as if the effort of mastication absorbed her entire being. My younger cousin, her long legs tucked under the table, licked the corners of her lips, her gaze fixed on the plate where the last two squid, stuffed with garlicky meat and flavored with tomato sauce, waited their turn to be devoured. She would gladly have tasted of the recalcitrant mollusk, just to pass the time (which went by slowly, so slowly on Sundays, between Potbelly and Southpaw, the ant and the cockroach, the First Prize for Virtue and the bogeyman). No one there to admire her long legs. Nutsandbolts had pried himself away after lunch. He wasn't exactly a head-turner, with his air of an old scout grinding away at his Kama Sutra, always on the watch and just dying to be rapped on the knuckles, but as a Sunday distraction in the kitchen gleaming with boredom, and as a guinea pig for fine-tuning her seduction techniques, the ersatz Zuricher would do just fine. So long as a male was prowling around the spanking new house, the atmosphere was charged with promising electricity (Big Sister started acting like a corporal ordering her troops onward, while Southpaw rubbed her chin with the end of her stump, gazing over those present with an alert eye, watching for the imminent bolt of lightning to strike the abode of happiness). And, in the middle of this trigon, the long legs came and went, describing frightful sinusoids that clouded the male's vision and made his spouse feel like puking. My younger cousin, having shed her blue ballet slippers, perched on her seat, bust arched forward, feet bare, her eyes darting from the thin mouth that meticulously ground the cephalopod to the stump resting against the sink and tracing haloes on the stainless steel edge. She lit a cigarette, pulled from the pack that swelled the pocket of the shirt she'd knotted at the waist. A grunt immediately sounded across from her, obliging the long legs to extricate themselves from beneath the table and head toward the garden door. With an energetic hand my older cousin waved off the offending volute. The empty dish, pocked with red sauce, was removed and passed under a spray of boiling water. At the door, the nymph smoked her cigarette with her back to the kitchen. She threw the butt into the grass and, her bare feet brushing the lawn, hands on hips, rocked her upper body back and forth, right and left. Fast in its barrette, her hair quivered on the nape of her neck. She stretched out an arm, took a deep breath, and pirouetted 180 degrees. (Seen from the garden, the kitchen gleamed with the same boredom. Southpaw had not moved from her place near the sink. With folded arms, she stared at Potbelly, bent over the freezer, absorbed in counting the hibernating squids and blocks of rock-hard meat. What a plague Sundays were, between the hot-air balloon and the deadwood!) If King Lear's vacation plans hadn't been on the agenda, Long Legs would have bailed some time ago. But no way to escape the boredom. Nor the emaciated oldster, who they'd have to extract from his dollhouse, pick up when he descended from the plane, and drag through the streets of the city. My younger cousin, yawning voluptuously, left the garden and approached the door to the kitchen. She paused on the threshold, admired her reflection in the glass, and lightly brushed off a speck clinging to her thigh. Her inventory of the supply chest complete, Potbelly had settled anew in her chair, her way of declaring the meeting back in session; but the beautiful brown legs tarried near the door, pleased with the image of their curves. Such long legs, made for prancing at the summit, and condemned, while waiting for the magic cavalcade to sound, to sliding into her cubicle, where they were seen only by the libidinous eyes of little telemarketers fallen on hard times and not about to clamber back up. A deep sigh made the body of the young colt go limp, bent under the weight of sudden and exhausting revelations about the mediocrity of existence. With surly mien, vacant stare, and sour puss, she returned to her place at the table and lengthily caressed her thighs, plucking up her courage by fingering her riches to gauge their velvety firmness—even though that very morning, as every Sunday, she had measured, with the red ribbon reserved for this function, the circumference of her pegs, carefully waxed before being anointed with almond milk. Pegs for which every virgin boy on earth would give up his soul, Theo had declared to the entire telemarketing firm. All the literature in the world for a young girl's thigh, Theo had also said, always keeping in reserve an expression he could pull from his sleeve. At the time, he was a god for the pretty young doll, whose heart went pitter-pat, anticipating all the miracles that would transfigure her monotonous days now that Theo had arrived—even if for the time being he'd donned the guise of a temp, occupied, as was she, with sorting those who ate of the can from those who partook of the frozen. The divine Theo spoke volubly and each of his words sent ants crawling up the pretty young doll's legs; she pranced, her eye dazzled by the gold dust wafting about Theo the snake-oil salesman, the juggler of dreams.

It was foretold that he would lift her from this pit in which her gorgeous gams had become mired, would wrest her from this keyboard on which she entered numbers at random and chatted up strangers who couldn't believe their good fortune; strangers who, while ticking off their preferences (*tea or coffee? toast or cereal? canned or frozen? briefs or boxers?*), complimented the telemarketer on her charming voice, which they liked *a lot, enormously,* as much as the frozen peas on the questionnaire. At the other end of the line, the doll played along, like a princess of the royal blood about to recover her crown, condescending to a few familiarities before taking wing toward the Elsewhere that Theo of the feverish mien outlined for her daily, breathing smoke and mirages. Theo the Big Shot had a long reach, you see, tentacular relations who asked only to be at his beck and call. If he just gave the word, the beautiful colt would gallop toward the high life, letting fly in passing kicks to the little telemarketers, a confraternity to which Theo belonged through a perverse quirk of fate that had commanded him to wash up on these shores just so he could rescue those stranded long legs. Thus spake Theo all through the night, spinning metaphors soaked in whiskey, and good whiskey at that, courtesy of the doll. She couldn't do enough for the kinglet, who had commandeered her gorgeous gams, along with the futon on which he contorted them into perilous figures of his own devising. Once his conquest of the perineum was assured, all that remained was to extend the area under his dominion. In no time at all, the conquistador settled into the attic studio on Rue Glacière, a fitting appellation judging by its tenant, who, after conceding the usual delights for the first few weeks, revealed herself to be mortally frigid. (The doll, as Theo liked to repeat to all and sundry, when parceling out her ardors, rarely let go a rattle. Her eel-like body writhed out of his grasp, her vulva slammed shut, her pointed breasts recoiled at his kneading, her gorgeous gams protected themselves from caresses with the disdain of ancient idols repulsed by profane gropings. The ice queen only gave it up for lingual homage—at which point, docile, she abandoned her body to the tongue of the conquistador, who groomed her from her ears down to her toes and, once the deeply incised vulvular slit had released its sap, went promenading along her spine before forcing its way, with little lapping and sucking sounds, into the secret entrance under the sacrum.) Said entrance at that very moment was itching my younger cousin, who, rocking on her chair, tugged on her shorts to stop the irritating sensation. She untied her hair, twisted a lock around her finger, and studied its fine point. Opposite her, big sister had laid on the table the pencil and notepad retrieved from the drawer beneath the sink. With calm hand she smoothed her blue-glinted hair, adjusted her bun, slid thumb and forefinger into an opening in her ample green silk blouse to straighten her bra, and, squinting slightly, reviewed the column of figures jotted down before the squid Provençal interlude. She ticked off the list while shooting sidelong glances toward the sink, where I'd been standing alone since they'd cleared the flowered table of its lunch plates and left the dining room—hubby standing, drapes puckered—to reconvene in the pantry; before his dominical retreat, the master of the house had insisted on giving a complete demonstration of the latest gear, including high-tech backpack, air purifier, ultrasound emitter that could fend off brigades of mosquitoes and other flying pests (but nothing to ward off the bad juju from the one-handed harpy). My cousin caressed her stomach as if to reassure the little prince and protect herself from the anathema and invectives that I was of course slyly honing in my corner, just waiting for the chance to shoot my bolt in her direction. Biting her lower lip, thin and tinted pale rose, my cousin mentally rechecked her calculations. King Lear's final consolation weighed a bit heavy on the bottom line. It's just that the wedding, the new house, the carefully selected furnishings, their electronic fancies embedded in genuine-looking antiques, had drained the river of gold that flowed in the bed of the wisdomseeker and his vigilant better half—who was now kicking herself for having thought of organizing this twentieth reunion. But the dramatic chord that had always vibrated in her now swelled in volume, impatient to make others hear its poignant little melody. The prospect of King Lear's holiday electrified her dreamy and provident, sentimental and pragmatic nature. Finally she could satisfy her love of tear-jerking ritual: as eldest, she alone would ensure its successful outcome and officiate over the congruous rhythm of effusions (or so she hoped). She had long awaited this ceremony commemorating their desertion. She could finally show King Lear that she'd made her own way, that she was heading straight down the path to supreme happiness, carrying on her back a spanking new house, in her belly a little prince, and under her arm an enlightened scoutmaster. She felt rise within her waves of pride, engulfing her in the thought of all that felicity, insured against every hazard and acquired with the wiles of a Sioux. The arrival of King Lear promised to be the crowning jewel of this honorable career. How could my cousin deny herself the eloquent spectacle of one generation greeting another—of the old man bowing before the little prince whose advent would send him cartwheeling into the grave? She was full of pep, now that the *little family* had begun gestating. For years she had pushed her hand truck through the fog: now the engine was starting to roll for good, and in the desired direction. Seeing her little convoy finally on the right track made her head spin and honed her philosophy of life, like a stationmaster eager to keep one train right behind the next, each speeding to make its final destination on time. From *his* final destination, King Lear, in his wobbling little wagon, was just a stone's throw. But at the other extremity of life, on the starting line, the little prince was already revving up his motor. And make no mistake, it was a first-class carriage that would run the wobbling wagon into the ditch. New generations flourish on tombs. As long as there's life, there's hope, my cousin enjoyed saying— she who, adjusting the dogma of metempsychosis to fit her philosophizing candor, believed firmly in a next life, a kind of remedial session in which the washouts of this existence would be granted another shot at the front ranks. The famous ranks that, in her desire for a reasonable but solid success, my cousin, unlike her flighty younger sister, had never draped in gold and glory, trusting exclusively in her snail-like antennae to find her a house and a little family to carry on her back. The same antennae advised her to keep a strict watch. No more indulgences. Not one more cent should exit the *little family*. Everything would go into the kitty, for the bright future of the little prince. From first cry to last sigh, from cradle to grave, everything would have to be managed well in advance. The expectant mother had been overcome by planning fever, and King Lear's visit was not included in her entertainment budget. Warm flushes followed by cold sweats alternately heated and chilled my cousin's blood when she tallied up the cost of this jaunt. But nothing in the world could have dissuaded her from her charitable enterprise, and budget be damned. For the ancestor's coming, my cousin wanted to bite the bullet and make several more extravagant purchases, enough to bring the spanking new house up to code as a residence of status, the design of which she had been studying in home improvement magazines—though lately these had been cast aside for manuals on the art of preparing a radiant future for little princes. As for Old Lear, once his travel expenses were met, on his arrival they would still have to attend to his accoutrement, dress him from head to foot, as tropical garb threatened to stand out like a sore thumb in the streets around here. And once he was grounded and trussed like a king, they would still need to find him distractions, titillate all his senses, and give him an eyeful before he shut his eyes for good. All that swank to ensure King Lear would have a grand old time. She deserved a medal, that good and gentle cousin of mine: wresting a smile out of the old piker would be no easy trick. And it wasn't even certain he'd take the bait, let himself be shod and dragged from the blue house all the way to the gleaming kitchen, then revived, spruced up, and seasoned to every taste, following the whims of these two fishwives who were beginning to squirm at the thought of being stuck with a mopey captive. King Lear wasn't what you'd call a talker. My younger cousin remembered this, though she'd only known him for the first few years of her life. For the last twenty, she had verified the accuracy of that old impression through the lapidary notes received and translated without further ado by her sister, who deplored their coldness of tone but congratulated herself on the fact that—their birth idiom having, as it were, evaporated from the younger one's brain—she had become their sole addressee, thereby taking her revenge on the years in the blue house when her seniority had failed to secure her first place in King Lear's heart. The old fool had fallen head over heels for the younger, who had not yet grown her long legs but already possessed a fine talent for bewitchment. Then the worm had turned. Now only the elder, who had not burnt any bridges but continued to burnish the memory of her native tongue, was up to deciphering King Lear's rebuses. Now she held the waning old man in her clutches; she of the pious disposition would light up his final days with this fabulous voyage. Tallying the column of figures that had just been rounded up by the plump sum they'd need for a week at the seashore, she became dizzy with the greatness of her own soul. My cousin liked the ocean. An atavistic passion. At least she had that much in common with the old man. Often in his letters he told of his excursions to Vung Tau. He caught the early bus, stayed in a fleabag hotel. Its windows looked out on the site where they were building a very classy saprophyte, which grew visibly, devouring the smaller houses around it. For some time now, the beach, too, had been going nouveau riche. Motorboats furrowed the horizon just off the cape. King Lear spent hours sitting on the sand, looking at the boats sparkling on the surface of the ocean. It had been a long time since he'd seen dinghies at Vung Tau. It brought back some queer memories. Twenty years before, he'd been sitting in the same spot, bare feet buried in the sand, watching the dinghies. It was the same sight, only more frantic. It was two weeks before the great debacle. The tocsin had sounded for the country's rich folk. The runaways crowded in from Saigon, which was about to fall at any minute, the latest arrivals said. They tried to assume the casual look of people who had just gone out for some fresh air, for a little ride in the outboard. In the middle of the night, shadows piled onto the dinghies and glided to boats waiting offshore to carry them far away from the plague then unfurling over Saigon. They left like thieves, without closing up their houses, emptying their pools, or parking the second car in the garage. Decamping at first light, in the big car sans chauffeur, they had arrived at Vung Tau, faces ashen and eyes ringed red, lips murmuring prayers to the god of the rich not to let them down, now that they'd abandoned to the Communists their villa with swimming pool, Chinese antiques, American bar, spying chauffeur, and shiftless servants. While waiting to embark on their canoe, they paced to and fro, rigid as sentinels. The women arched their backs, perched on shoes with dangerously high platform soles, the cavities of which were stuffed with jewelry. The men, eyes glued to the horizon, blended, for perhaps the last time, the smoke from their cigars with the ancestral dust. Occasionally they slid their hands beneath their jackets to finger the cash wadded inside, which could always double as a bulletproof vest if things turned even uglier. In Vung Tau, the rich were first in line to flee this land they had loved so well, which in return had fattened them up more than was good for them. The ship was sinking, the riffraff were at the gates—at least if King Lear were to believe his mother-in-law, who suddenly showed up at the blue house after years of scornful silence, broken only to bury the daughter who had died in childbirth, leaving her two orphanlets in the lurch. Their grandmother chose to see this premature demise as a redress of her witless daughter's ruinous marriage to King Lear, whose fortune was so pitiful that he couldn't even contribute to the funeral. It was Grand-mother who presided over such rites in that region, and in rap-tor's memory no jackal had ever known a juicier slaughterhouse. So after years of dismissive silence, Lady Jackal, now fleeing the country, made a detour to the blue house. She had to scram, and quick. She could smell the persistent whiff of riffraff in the air. She already imagined her head on a pike, her torso pickled, the rest thrown to the dogs. The bells in her ancestral altar had rung in the middle of the night. Then the god of the rich had come to her in a dream with a warning. At daybreak, she had assembled her troops and bundled the whole family into her huge sedan. But when they reached the outskirts of Saigon, the image of the two orphanlets had suddenly danced before her eyes. She had to res-cue them, had to save my little cousins. She had to wrest them away from King Lear, stuff them in the huge sedan already crammed with the children and grandchildren living under her bell jar. No sooner said than done. Lady Jackal appeared at the blue house and made off with my two cousins, who left, eyes shining with excite-ment, for an outing to the seashore and never returned. Several days after the kidnapping, King Lear received a large photo, brought by an itinerant photographer coming from Vung Tau, where the runaways indulged in the poor man's pleasure and paid double for pictures of their last squints in the ancestral homeland. The photo showed Lady Jackal, thin and dry, dressed in black silk, hair impeccably pulled back, lips taut, gaze fearless, facing away from the sea and surrounded by her entire brood. In the front row, at far left, my two cousins squeezed against each other, heads sunk down to their shoulders, looking like chicks tossed into a condor's nest. The little chicks took to the sea, in a motorboat that sliced through the night and brought them aboard a ship — the first leg of a flight to France, where Lady Jackal kept her real estate investments, her bank account, and a portion of her prog-eny, sent ahead as scouts. With the photo folded in four in his pocket, King Lear took the first bus for Vung Tau. He sat for two days and two nights looking out toward the ocean, bare feet buried in the sand, listening to the putt-putt of the dinghies that were waiting for cover of darkness to load on more runaways and pull away from shore. After the first week, the flood of large sedans slowed to a trickle. The abandoned dinghies bobbed on the water. The second week, the beach was deserted, the nights undisturbed. The bus no longer went to Vung Tau. King Lear had jostled in the rear of a Honda all the way back to Saigon, which the Communists had just entered.

Maybe we should forget the seashore, it might stir up too many things. My elder cousin was of a mind that we should make do with a week in the country instead. The prospect of picnic lunches in the grass and evenings around the fireplace in the middle of nowhere made the younger one wince: her long legs preferred the hot guys on the beach, no question about that. But, without a cent to her name, the nymph didn't have much say in the matter. All the gorgeous gams could do was prepare themselves, some beautiful autumn Sunday, for nourishing an ant colony. My younger cousin drew another cigarette from her pocket, holding it between her fingers, unlit, in a meditative pose, while musing out loud. A weekend at the Grand Hotel would be so much more fun. Or, for a walk on the wild side, how about a night out at an amusement park, like the one she'd seen in that black-and-white detective flick? She liked all that stuff: the shouts, the laughter, the lights, the crowds at the shooting galleries, at the automated fortune teller's, hands thrust into the mouth of truth. She'd go on the big merry-go-round, treat herself to a ride on the scenic railway. She'd eat cotton candy while singing *Yeah, I'll take you for a scenic ride, Don't make a face, you'll get your way, Yeah, I'll take you for a scenic ride, But feelings like that come cheap, Yeah, I'll do you on the scenic ride, yeah yeah yeah.* She'd wear a white pleated skirt that would billow up, and whichever way she turned dozens of eyes would be there devouring her whole. The hall of mirrors would send back the distorted image of an enchantress whose rancor was starting to gnaw away at her. For now, the nymph cultivated her childlike spirit, pampered her sure-fire kisser, so soft to the touch, all her mishaps having only inverted the curve of her mouth, which now traced a falling crescent moon. Every morning, before the bathroom mirror in the Rue Glacière studio, she repeated the same gesture: raising her fingers in a V and poking them into the corners of her lips to jerk them upward. But the crescent moon always fell back down and the same film of frustration covered her puss. Theo the magician, with the tip of his magic wand, had raised a tornado of hope that soon scattered into bitter dust, an insidious dust that irritated the nymph's eyes, darkened her complexion, clogged up her reveries, dulled down her days—which already seemed like a row of drab little pebbles, arranged in banal patterns by a lusterless destiny. But even so, she still couldn't keep from hoping. Something would show up, deal her a new hand. She was betting on the arrival of King Lear. Even if, for now, the prospect of the reunion basically bored her silly, such an event couldn't help rattling her to the core, tinting the uniform pebbles a pretty pink. And the bitter dust, which had settled in the bed of her heart, would be swept away. She pondered all these thoughts, her gaze somnolent, fingers bending the cigarette that she still had not lit and that now snapped in two. She took the pieces and meticulously shredded the paper, spilling all the tobacco on the table, which she then gathered up in a little pile, then divided in two, then again in two, before forming the pile again, then once more dividing it into a different pattern, and so on, all with hypnotic slowness, while across the table her sister uttered numbers and figures in a monotonous voice, at regular intervals, like a leaky faucet. Drowsiness oozed over the gleaming kitchen. Her elbow on the table propping up her head, my younger cousin rubbed her nose, eyes half shut, lower lip pouting. Only a few more hours of this to endure. With a little luck, the Sunday meditator would come home from his prayer center before dinnertime. Meanwhile, the atmosphere was dull, the air lacking in spice. Another lousy Sunday, crushed between Potbelly and Southpaw—and there she was, scratching her stump again. She did that every time someone looked at her. With less conviction, it seemed. She must have been holding in her prophesying frenzy. Saving some for this evening at the dinner table: it would be more disgusting and more spectacular. One more storm and the single-handed sibyl would be in seventh heaven, from where she hoped to witness the promised ruination. She played at being pure, an Antigone, a Cassandra, the whole virginal menagerie—though in that regard, she was more like an immaculate catacomb. Her closets were full of skeletons, but verboten to go rummaging through the back alleys of her guilty conscience. She never said a word about it. The cripple played it close to the vest and lectured everybody else. *You should leave King Lear alone,* she chided, draped in her dark clothes, the baggy trousers and bulky cardigans that didn't even make her sweat. There was something wrong with a body that never perspired, never let anything out. She could really get on your nerves, always hovering about, with her air of omniscience, her crudely chopped hair, her Miss I-Know-Misery manner, and her stump that crept up without warning to poke you in the back, just between your shoulder blades. It was enough to make you shriek out loud. And even that was nothing compared with her mini-dramas. Like the time she came banging at the door of Rue Glacière in the middle of the night, her face, neck, and hands covered in blood. She was still clutching the razorblade. Her hand, forehead, and throat were slashed up good, though when you looked more closely, the cuts were only superficial. Not even enough to make a kitten bleed to death. The bitch had been very careful not to touch her face. Just some light gashes on her forehead, like sanguine wrinkles. She'd done herself up staring calmly into the bathroom mirror, her stump resting on the edge of the sink, the fingers of her right hand not even trembling as they pinched the blade. Once she'd given her new look its finishing touches and gauged the effect in the glass, she just had to run over and bang at the door of Rue Glacière. There she was, on the landing, lit by the dim hallway bulb. There she was, with her ecstatic martyr face, that red necklace around her collar and all that caked blood on her forehead, as if she'd lost her crown of thorns en route. Little cousin had had to take care of her, weep over her cruel disfigurement, shed tears of pity and fear. And all the while, the bitch was solid stone, with the look of someone who knew all about unhappiness; who spat on life's everyday pleasures; who every morning breathed in the toxic vapors seeping from the major brains aligned on the shelf above her bed, then spent her nights raveling and unraveling the cloth of her grief— a grief of superior vintage, the kind you learn in books, *whoamIwhereamIgoingwhatamIdoingtowhatpurpose,* a whole rosary of cavils. Enough to max out your burden of woes, just in case you were tempted to feel carefree for a moment, and to sock you with a good downer for the rest of your life. With Southpaw, it was a special kind of grief, more like a depressive mope, a corpse-like arrogance. When the three of them got together on Sundays, she always stayed in her corner, stiff as a statue. The sort of person, with her sermons and prophecies, to send you leaping into the flames of remorse, without lifting so much as a finger. She had kept her scars for weeks, especially around her neck. She had bought a red scarf, wearing it so that they were all you saw—the young lady enjoyed a whiff of danger now and then! And danger made her look superb and bruised, which actually suited her rather well, even lent her martyr act some depth. She always found a way to pass herself off as the poor soul. Whereas when you thought about it, she had it pretty sweet. With her disability pension that left her scads of free time, she had nothing better to do than twist her brain in knots, try to ratchet up her unhappiness to vindicate the lugubrious minds aligned above her bed. Unbalanced minds, who exhaled their cadaverous breath on her. She drove everyone to distraction

with her obsessive worst-case scenarios and doom-and-gloom sermons. A little nudge toward the abyss, just in case you still had
too much get up and go to awake one morning and notice that
nothing had changed overnight, that your burden still weighed
like lead. Except that at seventeen, the little soldier's kitbag had
been stuffed with dreams. Back then you could believe you'd end
up clawing your way to the summit to plant your flag; but after
falling down so many times, you lost your standard; and now you
just hoped to cling to something halfway up, because illusions had
turned to bitterness and bitterness could cut you off at the knees.
Disappointment was the only lesson this life had to offer. But
where was the mainspring hidden, the one that made you get up
with the alarm and go catch the bus to the telemarketing firm, then
the elevator that went up to the office for little telemarketers, then
the elevator that went back down to the cafeteria for little telemarketers and that once in a while stopped at the mezzanine, where
around the coffee machine the little telemarketers plotted a radiant future? It was just talk, in any case, for given the way things
looked (and the sharpest little telemarketers all agreed that things
didn't look good), it was better to toe the line, while waiting for
the gong of fate to sound. A piercing shriek shook the kitchen from
its drowsy fog, restoring it to its dominical gleam. My younger
cousin raised her head, tousled her hair, brushing away with an
abrupt wave the parade of regrets that dulled her skin. Opposite
her, eye still glazed by the round of figures dancing to the tune of
the piggybank lullaby, my older cousin jumped up and, fixing her
falling bun, headed toward the exposed brick portion of wall, in
which a large oven was embedded, equipped with a handle and
fat chrome knobs. It was something old refurbished for today's
tastes, and its clock emitted long shrill whistles at regular intervals that one halted by hammering the oven's impassive front; a
few vigorous bangs immediately restored silence in the pantry. My
cousin heaved a sigh, leaned back against the oven, and rubbed
her eyes. She stretched, massaged her neck, laid her hand on her

belly with a yawn. She felt like resting on the English sofa bed bought for King Lear and temporarily installed in the dining room. She always lay down there in the afternoon to study manuals on the art of preparing radiant futures for little princes. If we would kindly follow her, my younger cousin and I, the discussion could resume in the queen's salon: she loved nothing better than to draw up battle plans and assign each one her place in the imminent upheaval, all the while reclining in a languid pose. In her condition, she had every right. And besides, with her deep pockets and sharp tongue, power was hers de facto. If it weren't for the queen, the ancestor could squat forever in his ruined palace and his other daughter would just sit there, crossing and uncrossing her gorgeous gams, heaving sighs that spoke volumes about her impotent melancholy. However she looked at it, the queen saw herself being offered proof of her indispensability at the crucial moment: guardian of the treasure, keeper of the open sesame, without whom King Lear's epistolary blathering would remain a dead letter, and the prospect of a reunion lost in the dense clouds where the long-legged dreamer built her castles. My elder cousin had had the foresight to hoard everything, her local currency and that fading dialect. She'd learned that lesson from her grandmother. Once you had the good end of the stick, you had to hold onto it, let nothing slip your grasp, wrap everything tight, old and new, following the law of maximum retention. This was the first commandment of Lady Jackal, who was no longer with them to bless this respect for her precepts, observed with fanatical devotion— to the point where everything in the new household, from the cookbooks to the mistress's impeccable chignon, looked as if it had been placed there in homage to the departed Lady. In the midst of all this cutting-edge comfort, the flame of tradition burned bright, tended by the potbellied vestal—all the more zealously in that, when it came to stoking the fire of their origins, she could hardly count on Southpaw or Long Legs. (They had taken a powder long ago. First-class deserters, those two! Busily snuffing out the fire and grinding the ashes underfoot to keep from getting caught. Try as you might to titillate their roots, you wouldn't get a rise. Southpaw resisted the desire to scratch her stump by plunging into one of those books she always lugged around in her pockets. Long Legs, meanwhile, with a faint nervous tic, cast about for the exit—quick, before this confab turned into a stranglehold.) At the end of the day, my cousin was all alone, with her round belly, solid head, and well-anchored heart; alone in tending her beautiful, healthy, hearty roots. (In contrast to the sickly stock that poisoned Southpaw and the floating radicles that writhed around Long Legs. It was pitiful to see that pair of lost souls, one dizzier than the other. Sometimes they were like sinister ghost trains that had derailed, sometimes like tops spinning uncontrollably on water. One day it was deep sorrow, the next sheer indifference. With their busted compasses, it was all they had—pure childishness, an unhappy-making spectacle.) Before which my cousin of the rounded belly and solid roots congratulated herself on having the battened-down good sense to dismiss vain sorrow and rise to the occasion, while the two little ninnies blew back and forth between shame and disdain, remorse and effrontery, as right now when they were left by themselves, face to face in the gleaming kitchen.

I lingered near the sink, drinking a tall glass of water. My younger cousin scooped the tobacco on the tabletop into the palm of her hand, then went to throw it out in the garbage pail under the sink. She filled a glass of water for herself, downing it in one gulp. A damp pearl shone on her lower lip. Her hand slid nimbly into the pocket of my jacket and pulled out the small volume I'd brought with me. She opened it at random and began reading, eyes open wide, like a pupil hungry for knowledge. When the cutie waved her pennants like that, the smartest thing the targeted adversary could do was gather her wits to ward off the imminent charm offensive. The cutie's tactic was endlessly renewable and high-yield.

She herself couldn't get over how well it worked, every time: it would have taken a lot more than that to pull one over on *her*. Never, had she been a bit luckier, would anyone have made her give up the goods with just some sweet little nothings. Then again.... Come to think of it, Theo the teetering god had done a pretty good job of stripping her bare. For thirty-six months she'd been giving him bed and board, in exchange for grand tirades about singing tomorrows; but mornings continued to rise on the attic studio that reeked of piss from the cat taken in late last year to act as mediator, since these days Theo the unmasked enchanter got knocked back on his ass whenever he tried to vaunt the power of his magic wand to his darling. She'd rather talk to the cat, which listened, phlegmatic, to both sides, and received from each enough petting to overload its little heart. Now that the scales had fallen from her eyes and the feline's company proved multiply advantageous, my cousin was pondering how to dislodge her parasitic deity—who, once secure in his hold on the attic studio, had deserted the ranks of the little telemarketers to rehash his get-rich-quick schemes fulltime. While waiting for the great strategist to unearth a ladder of sufficient height, one naturally had to provide his accommodations, not to mention his whiskey, the daily absorption of which was eliminated around nightfall in effusions of grandeur and a stream of fantabulous promises. In order to twiddle his thumbs in peace while nurturing his battle plan, the sodden strategist had found nothing better than to send his darling, for a few more months, just a few more, back to the telemarketing firm. And my cousin had had no problem with that. The main thing was not to let loose the hem of her god, whom she could certainly relieve of life's practicalities while he counted his chickens, sucking on the teat of Johnnie Walker, splayed out on the futon like a megalomaniacal tick. She had put her heart and soul into it. The valiant girl got up at the crack of dawn, rushed to the office, worked overtime, and came home late, her arms laden with the shopping she'd done on the fly during lunch break instead of going down to the caf, where the little telemarketers plotted to loosen ever so slightly the shackles that kept them from spreading their wings and flying away, smashing holes in the office windows as they went. Question from telemarketer soaring in air to passer-by dazed with sleep but rushing to put her head in the yoke one more day: *Have you ever taken flight? Never—sometimes—rarely. Under what circumstances have you had occasion to fly? To escape the office? The car? The subway? The family table? The marriage bed? Your phenomenal solitude?* My cousin didn't give a fig about flying away. She wasn't one for schoolgirl utopias, moth-eaten little escapes. Even with her feet firmly on the ground, she could soar high with her long legs, now that she'd found them a manager. She just needed patience. To whet her appetite, every evening Theo the manager unveiled his grandiose schemes, his mouth full of delicacies prepared by the darling who, the minute she walked in the door, got busy in her corner kitchenette. Theo's voice covered the hiss of sizzling meats. The manager didn't skimp on special effects. One day, spotlights swept with a supernatural glow a newly built production outfit (the gorgeous gams should be in pictures, that went without saying), but the next day, at the same happy hour, the décor of the production outfit had been hauled away to make room for a talent agency. No bullshit this time. Theo had just run into a Big Noise, with whom he'd been matey-matey before washing up at the telemarketing firm. The Big Noise wanted in on the deal. On the financial backing for the talent agency. All they had to do now was put the gorgeous gams on the market. After that, sayonara attic studio with futon and hotplate. Theo would wrest from the earth castles made-to-measure for his princess. She only had to choose her model from the magician's extensive catalogue. A penthouse. Better yet, a small townhouse, for just the two of them, renovated floor to ceiling, roof to garden, and parked in front of it two cars, one large and very chic, the other a little coupe, cute as a button, perfect for leggy effects. The prestidigitator's empires rose at aperitif time, only to deflate once the dawn bugle sounded. The gorgeous gams resumed their stations of the cross to the telemarketing firm. But back then nothing could shake my cousin's faith; she believed firmly in those mirages and slaved in anticipation of her triumph. It took two whole years for Darling to come down from the drunkard's speechifying. In the twelve months after that, the parasitic god leeched onto his lost paradise with the tenacity of a tapeworm. But while he still found it convenient to squat on the left half of the futon, which an invisible sword had severed from the right, one by one he saw all the pleasures of Eden fall away. Johnnie Walker ran dry. The Frigidaire stood empty. Darling still came home just as late, but only after having taken sustenance in the company of some little telemarketer on a spree. And there you had it! War is hell. To each his own trench. Too bad for Cupid's bloody corpse, ravaged by Spanish fly. After two years of artificial paradises and scratching each other's backs, they'd reached the point of daggers drawn, ready to retool each other's hides with a kris—when they cared enough, and they didn't care enough very often, because indifference, with its chalk mask, its dull gazes, its fine wrinkles of disgust at the corners of the mouth, had inevitably set up camp. Indifference always gained the whip hand in the final account. After the emotions, the daggers grew dull, too. Why bother unsheathing them? It wouldn't budge the lump sitting opposite her by a centimeter. You might as well walk over him. Trip over the flotsam of happiness. Remnants of the sacked god lay all about the attic studio. My cousin kicked them aside on her way out, wiped her feet on them when she came home. The screaming and shouting left a pleasant echo. But the lump hadn't said his final word. There were still a few fits and starts, devised in the silence of the attic where the recently acquired cat prowled, and where the phone had been cut off: Darling refused flat out to pay for the unproductive deliria that the buccaneer drooled into the receiver, stroking the fur of the second secretary to the Big Noise, who purred at the other end of the line just like the cat accepting his caresses with princely indolence. The place stank of disaster. The parasite was ordered to vacate the premises and, until then, to put a lid on his megalomaniacal tirades. Time for the old ham to find a new routine. The tide of fabulous promises ebbed, ushering in a torrent of tears and hiccupped wailing that washed over my cousin the moment she returned. No more bluffing. Out came the violins and hankies. The curtain rose on a cacophony of tremolos and sniveling. The ham pulled out all the stops, eyes bloodshot, cheeks sallow, breathing heavy, his old silk shirt all rumpled and open to his bellybutton, his flannel jacket smeared with grease stains, one foot in a worn slipper, the other in a black silk sock, cigarette trembling at the corner of his lips. The full regalia of the magnificent loser, doomed to fall, swimming against the tide of petty ambitions, beating his head against a wall of incomprehension. Now that his magic tricks had flopped, Theo opted for fragility, ran daily through his evening vespers, pumped up by his latest psychological discovery—to wit, that with dolls you first had to appeal to their thirst for glory, then, when that stopped working, to their charitable sentiments, their instinct for consolation, their mania for redemption. Nothing better than fate's walking wounded to stimulate the little nightingales' tear ducts. Just make as if to fall and they stretched out their hand. To see themselves in your tiny, terror-stricken hound dog eyes and tell themselves that, all things considered, they deserved some credit. You were supposed to pave them a shortcut to the good life and now they were the ones picking *you* up. If you could lay on the appalling contortions a bit thicker, spew out your repentance along with your snot, they'd faint with emotion. Basically, there's no big secret to being with a doll. When they stop buying your bluffs, you just let them despise you a bit. It elevates them. And, from the heights of their regained self-esteem, they look at you like a broken old toy that they've glued back together but that they could crush at any moment with just a squeeze of their delicate little fingers. A broken old toy is still better than none. You whisper that in their ear, so they can toss it over a bit—now that you've built them a stucco pedestal, groveled at their feet, opened the tear ducts in their honor, devised thirty new daily variations on sighing, and reserved for those little vixens some prime tremolos. They won't just drop you, now that the show has been tweaked to perfection. Let them imagine for a moment the empty studio, without the doggy eating out of their hand. Without the whimpers of the sacked potentate. Nothing but silence, solitude, and the cold. And, to ward off the shadows, a little telemarketer now and again. A sensible transient with anemic imagination, his fantasy tank perpetually empty, barely able to feign a little inventiveness when it came to the in-and-out. He'd have to mobilize all his tawdry inspiration for the exploit. Then the minor miracle worker would roll over on his back for a sonorous repose, leaving the doll to lie there, wide eyes staring at the ceiling, listening to the Little Engine that Couldn't whistle with stentorian vigor as it departed for deep sleep and breathing in the odor of goat piss that's been hovering in the room since the sorcerer's apprentice ardently yanked off his socks. Might as well keep the nice doggy, his familiar sweat, his peepers that flare at the drop of a hat, his oral cavity that disgorges, for the sole pleasure of his singular audience, floods of delirium and pain. Thus whimpered the begging doggy, a bit dazed by the intensity of his palinodic cogitations but firmly resolved not to give up the floor. The insinuating Theo tended toward the unctuous and ingratiating. He was submission itself, dripping with honey and holy oil. The ploy worked like a charm. The lump, in mid-levitation, underwent a complete palingenesis. The invisible sword that had cloven the futon in twain flew away. As in the very first days, Theo had dominion over the gorgeous gams, which had grown a bit weary of abstinence and were ready to execute, in the wee hours, a few impure figures, posterior undulations included. For which every doggy on earth would give up his soul. Theo damned himself that much and more. But with dolls, you never knew what tomorrow would bring. For two nights running, the attic studio was pandemonium itself, and Theo the precarious victor roared, his snout nuzzling the reconquered territory, his muzzle sniffing ecstatically at his good fortune, his paws imprinting their tackiness on every square inch of the abandoned flesh. By the third day, the saturnalia was but a distant memory. The gorgeous gams, in a surge of dignity, had folded back into a fierce self-possession, and Rue Glacière again merited its name. The attic studio once again looked like a fallow field and, beneath the vellum of bitterness and bile, Theo and his darling, drawing faster than lightning, fired off their rediscovered rancor white-hot. And off for another round. The thresher cranked up again, the pipe-dream compactor creaked its gears, and shards of illusions shot into their bodies like shrapnel. The whole thing promised a nice case of gangrene. Purulent hatred. A thick scab of black moods. And to top it off, a lovectomy. A rapid and painless ablation, after which each one repaired to his corner, nerves deadened but once more master of his systoles. That's all my cousin was waiting for—for the invisible sword to make a clean slice, rid her once and for all of the doggy who could no longer even bark one of his up-the-sleeve formulas, the sort that melts doll-like hearts. The bell tolled, irrevocably. But just as he set off down the path of banishment, Theo was saved by one final, dramatic twist. The two nights in which Darling had fallen back under the sway of the toppled god left their mark. A seed germinated in the belly of the relapsed heretic. Theo the banished, called back in extremis, almost buckled under the emotion. The luck of a tapeworm, that one! There it was, his new role, handed him on a platter. The doggy could cling to the floor and change his routine. He was already drooling with paternity. The fiery orifice resumed spitting out promises and pipe dreams. The great god Theo had clambered back up his pedestal, while waiting to enthrone his heir apparent. But Darling didn't see things quite the same way. The order of banishment had not been rescinded; the accomplice had been dragged back by his shirttails merely to devise a quick plan for doing away with the body of the crime. Theo took this uppercut without flinching. The main thing was to obtain a reprieve and, for a few weeks more, attach his trematode suckers to the den of love. Not to mention that, opportunity making the thief, Theo quickly transmuted his nebulous hopes for paternity into a heroic and resolute anticipation of the tragedy about to befall him, depriving him of his posterity, but restoring some sheen to his magnificent loser's costume. Theo's mouth gushed boiling floods—promises and complaints— Darling didn't need to fret. Theo the great protector was there; he would swallow his paternal pride and find the shekels needed to uproot his progeny, since the little telemarketer, no longer up for the job, now brought in mere bagatelles, immediately frittered away on trifles. This time, Theo would rise to the occasion. Even if he had to throttle the flesh of his flesh with his own hands. Thus spake Theo the pathetic. But the days passed, the rent went unpaid, and the doll, still burdened, had no choice but to go make doe eyes at her cousin Southpaw that Sunday afternoon, taking advantage of a moment when they were alone, side by side at the gleaming sink in the spanking new house.

My cousin leafed through the book she'd lifted from my pocket and laid flat next to the sink. She nibbled on scraps of sentences, her head bent toward the open page, hair gathered to the left side of her face. From behind the black cataract stifled guffaws escaped like cat sneezes, by which my cousin manifested her interest, having heard tell that snickers were all the rage among subtle minds and that a snickering cutie was doubly cute, since it meant the devil had burrowed into her brain. But the devil didn't speak loudly enough to drown out the tweeting that continually peeped through, flooding her brain in a torrent of minuscule woes. The encephalic cheeping interfered with the vacillating baby bird's receptors as she draped her transitory interest for someone else in smiles and bobbed her head toward the bits of sentence to be pecked at (*once the animal feels the thread of its existence blocked, interrupted, light begins appearing constantly, like lightning on a summer's eve*). The next moment, her brain was already swelling with the rumbling of its woes (*that bikini wasn't bad but too expensive the bottom is cut high and shows off your legs but really too expensive*). One by one, the pecked-at phrases (*in this light shines the animal's entire future: in its pursuit of another animal, the chance to eat, sleep, drink, and nest*) were covered by the overflow of futile bitterness, until the sludge of little miseries stifled the heart and brain of the baby bird, who gave in and dragged her wings through the dung of her reveries (*have to wait until I have some cash but summer's almost over and next year one-pieces will be back in style sure as shooting and besides this is no time to go dipping into the kitty it's already leaking like a sieve*). Austerity was de rigueur, as long as her belly threatened to swell, like the queen reclining on the English sofa bed in the next room. Two of the favored, rowing like galley slaves toward the promised land of domestic bliss— the sight could move you to tears, but no way were the gorgeous gams going to let this ill-conceived dome grow and press its vile weight on her slender columns. She had to move fast, empty the abscess, cleanse her entrails. Southpaw asked nothing better than to help out. Her stump was already starting to itch, tingling with excitement at the prospect of being party to a nefarious scheme. Her lone hand tripped over itself in its rush to pull out the bills that would help purify the matrix, restoring Cutie's body to its fidgety suppleness and its desire to gambol, which, money on it, would take her far, once she had purged Theo the mirage-dealer and his germinating imposter, expelling both from their haven with a single heave-ho. The beauty was determined to give herself a complete makeover for the arrival of King Lear, who shouldn't have to see that, the parasite in her lair and his seed in her womb. She was going to decontaminate her body, dredge her head, re-gain her dominion over the attic studio, sweep out the shards of Theo the pulverized god, and, now redeemed, await King Lear in the pose of a frozen idol. For frozen she was. In any case, she didn't mind thinking she wasn't quite all there, that she was missing a duct, a reservoir of tears, a well to be tapped. Otherwise, how could one explain why she remained ice-cold whenever she tried to pour out her heart? She sniffled, batted her eyelids, pinched her arms, but something jammed up the works and her heart lay unmoved in its casket of ice. At most, if she bit her lip until it drew blood, she might manage a few droplets on her wintry cheeks. Never was a crybaby. She didn't want to look like a crushed tomato, with the red puffy eyes of a sleeping vampire, twisted mouth boohoohooing, nostrils oozing warm snot. Still, while Cutie balked at the idea of giving herself a tomato face, she knew what advantages could come with tears. She had taught herself to weep, just enough so as not to puff up her cute puss, while affecting a pained indifference. In such cases, she didn't even care how she looked: a loose lock of hair might fall onto her pouting lip, a raised corner of her skirt brush the top of her thigh. She wept with head held straight, eyes fixed on a point that, by her calculations, should be situated at a distance of exactly three paces, her rehearsals in the mirror having demonstrated that when her misty gaze focused on a point short of the mark, it made her look like a simpleton, whereas if her moist eyes strayed past the goal line she took on an ecstatic aura that ruined the effect. And this particular effect she had no intention of forcing. She had realized early on that, as much as she might twist and turn her thread of mercy, it wouldn't wring out a single tear. But far be it from the gorgeous gams to let slip even a hint that their silken attractions harbored steely blades, so shed tears she must. Now, the only thing that brought them to her eyes was thinking of the gorgeous gams' inevitable ruin—gams meant to frolic joyously but already mired in the ruts of defeat. Cutie didn't have the most developed sense of altruism—which made her no different from anyone else, and that was fine with her—but so long as counterfeit remained common coin, she had no choice in the matter. She had to find a lever to open the floodgates. She had taken her determination in both hands and set it loose on the question, answered in no time flat: since only self-pity stimulated her tear ducts, she just had to hone it, at the right moment, with extended reveries about her own death—a Technicolor movie of her burial, which she would attend as an invisible and privileged guest. All things considered, she deserved a gold medal for having pulled that one out of her hat: it had helped the little glacier send hot, salty pearls cascading down her cheeks, whenever circumstances called for her to manifest her concern with some demonstrative sobbing. Like the night Southpaw showed up after redecorating her witchy face with a razor. Miss I've-Got-Misery-in-My-Veins was capable of anything, to prove how deeply she'd dug through the rubble of her soul. She had knocked in the middle of the night at the studio door, so very eager to teach her younger cousin a lesson in morbidity—her cousin whose innocent head was clogged with whimsy and fairytales, the doll who dreamed only of curling up her long legs and returning to her cot, to suck her thumb while her acolytes leaned over her angel's bed and heaved oohs and ahs at the marvel before them. Just as they would bow in mute affliction before the glass coffin in which she saw herself lying, in a long white robe with lovely folds showing off the curve of her legs, removed from the acolytes' view as punishment for their having let such divine limbs muck about in the soil of petty life, where every day the price of everything rose: coffee and cigarettes, cat food and telemarketers' lunches. Thanks to those images of her funeral, the innocent had been able to sniffle that night for Southpaw, who wasn't as hideous as she tried to make out when she banged at the studio door like a bat, with just her razor-slashed head sticking out from her scarf and long black cape. The bat imagined she'd won the match, that she'd finally insinuated a little strain of unhappiness into the canary's brain. And how well the pretty birdie whistled the tune of compassion! She hopped all around the bat, examining its wounds with moist eyes, and even offering up half her nest. The bat removed its long black cape and lay down on the futon, next to the canary, who drifted to sleep with copious whimpers, moved to tears by the charitable action that rendered the princess in her glass coffin even more lovely. Except that a canary lying next to a bat didn't quite rest easy. The comely birdlet awoke with a start, shaking all over. It felt on its neck the icy breath of the noctule, who was surely plotting to smother the pretty sparrow with its long black cape, its flaccid wings, spread out for now at the foot of the bed. It gave the innocent birdie the cold sweats, now that she'd recovered from her burst of compassion. She rolled onto her back and lay still, eyes wide open in the dark. She had to fight against the sand stinging her eyes. That was the trap. Southpaw had slapped together her bloody makeover to allay her suspicions. The sight of all those small cuts on the patient's sad kisser made her head spin—she who was so delicate, who choked with rage on mornings when the bathroom mirror revealed the insidious emergence of a pimple threatening to ruin her flowerlike face. And here she was, lying in bed next to the wounded bat, who was sleeping or pretending to sleep, her black sweater open on a chest that had grown milky white from avoiding the sun. In the dark, the rose-colored scratches and smears of dried blood shone on her skin like traces of strawberry on whipped cream. It made you want to venture your tongue for a lick. But just at that moment, Southpaw moved in her sleep; her left arm rested across her face, hiding her eyes, leaving her stump hanging out—nice! A real stomach-turner. Revulsion surfaced anew. The cream had soured, the red strawberry traces smelled of rot, the stump offered itself in close-up with its grayish scar, its sutured skin, like a bone to suck on.

The ants started gnawing at my left extremity again: they rushed about, appetites whetted by the faint odor of disaster hovering above the gleaming kitchen, mixed with wafts of domestic harmony. A faint little odor, which barely tickled your nostrils. My cousins didn't suspect a thing. In the next room, on the English sofa bed, Potbelly was letting herself be lulled to sleep by the little prince's kicks. The long legs were way too long to feel the ground quake under their feet or the catastrophe descending upon the spanking new house. And, for the moment, the owner of the gorgeous gams felt more like wiggling, thrilled at having skirted her great peril. In exchange for a few moist bats of the eyelashes, she had managed to pry from Southpaw the necessary cash for relieving the burden that threatened to swell the Cutie, transforming her into an ambulatory mushroom with cloven hooves. The long legs moved away from the sink, where the book lay forgotten now that the trick had been performed, spitting out the pecked-at phrases with a grimace of disgust. Still, those phrases, which spun your head around, were far from lost. Southpaw had stirred them regularly and served them up again in her sermonizing voice that never lost a chance to crush your spirit — to scratch just where it was raw, to whisper in your ear words that you really didn't need to have burrowing in your brain. Words to make you think you'd found your way out, when you were merely running in blind circles around the mousetrap. A squirm here, a fidget there, and when you finally see a faint glow in the distance you hurtle toward it, rush forward with your precious, if slightly tarnished, flesh, only to find yourself caught in a box of maggots. To hear her tell it, your only choice was to fold up the gorgeous gams and sit there, head in hands, waiting for lightning to strike your skull or the maggots to gnaw your feet. And she was right to lie low, with that stump hanging from the sleeve of her jacket; but the long legs had been designed expressly to dance a jig under the eyes of her tamers. So when Southpaw recited her litanies, the owner of the gorgeous gams (not really one for ruminations that strained the brain) buried her head in her arms, rounded her back like a submissive sheep, and plunged into sweet dreams, where hot guys circled around her, mouths drooling and eyes shining greedily, to the rhythm of the muffled preaching. Did the sermons always have to pour into the same funnel—ears cute enough to nibble, made to be tickled night and day by compliments; ears equipped with a self-cleaning system that brushed out encrusted sermons; ears ready to start buzzing at the first sign of a stranglehold? And Southpaw wouldn't let it drop, always ready to empty her sack of bile, her pockets of pus, her reservoirs of black humors. Nothing to be done. She never gave up the goods without throwing in an extra sermon about the end of everything. As if Long Legs wasn't in enough of a tizzy as it was. Getting tugged between alpha and omega to boot. Sitting in a corner of the sun-drenched kitchen, her blue ballet slippers next to bare feet that wiggled their toes impatiently, my younger cousin, taking advantage of a pause in the rapid-fire sermons, abruptly raised her head from her arms. She stifled a yawn, shook out her hair, smoothed it, then, leaping up, leaned out the garden door and inhaled deeply, tugged on the cutoff jeans that were striping her rosy cheeks, spun on her heels, and, before returning to the shadows, smiled at her reflection in the windowpane, her pretty puss over which all this preaching (thank God!) had slid without leaving any trace but a light crease of sleep. A large ant, running over the collar of her shirt, hurtled down the left swell, descended to the shirttails knotted at her waist, disappeared into the folds and wrinkles, then scaled back up the row of buttons and slipped under the spotless fabric. The pretty puss took on an enraged grimace. My cousin shoved two fingers down her neckline in hot pursuit, but the indelicate beast had veered off toward her navel. Cursing and stamping her feet, my cousin undid the knot, shook out her shirt-tails, lifted them, clapped her hand on her nude belly and flicked off the intruder, which rolled to the ground and was immediately smushed by a furious toe. She retracted her foot, tucked in the tails of her shirt that puffed out her shorts, and graced the insect's corpse with a vengeful smile before nudging it with her toenail toward the lawn. A grunt sounded behind her. My older cousin, risen from her nap, stood at the kitchen door; her frowning eyes followed the brown smear the crushed ant left as it returned to its native habitat. *I dreamt about Grandmother,* she said, her eyes still fixed on the stain, as if the soul of the departed Lady had infiltrated the mangled body of the large ant. *Grandmother was lying in a drawer at the morgue, knitting her brow.* The knit in the dead woman's brow had come unstuck from between her eyes to go lodge between my cousin's. In her sleep, she had let her head be gobbled up by Grandmother's ghost, who had seized the opportunity to graft her pinched, haughty mien onto the sleeper's excoriated face. That's how the Lady had returned among us, with her impeccable chignon, thin lips, and pearl-studded ears, those precious pearls that she had bequeathed to the most promising chick in the brood. My cousin, starting awake from her nap, had risen from the English sofa bed and gone straight into her bedroom to rummage in the jewel box and take out the jackal's baubles, which she affixed to her earlobes. Grandmother was there, in the box's small mirror, with her bare dangling lobes, her eyes that, when they looked you up and down, literally sliced you in two. Grandmother frowned. She recalled the one time she had seen those pearls on my cousin's ears: the evening when she'd *croaked.* She was lying in her bed, not even washed or changed, in her ratty nightgown that had stunk like a shroud for days. She heard whispering outside the door. Lady Raptor's little brood was holding council in the living room. A hand turned the knob, then released it just as quickly. No one entered. She waited. Her mouth stretched like a serpent that had let go its prey. Her lids weighed on her razor-sharp eyes, now condemned to rust in their sheath. The condor called to her brood in a breathless voice, shouted with all the might of her despotic soul, but no one answered. The little ones whispered in the anteroom, murmured in each other's ears, pushed each other forward, trying to be the last to go in. But no one came. There were some footsteps, a nervous cough, the doorknob moved, then everything grew still again. The condor yelled louder. The little miscreants continued to peep as if they hadn't heard a thing. Suddenly, one of them piped up, *She's kicked it.* And the other two guffawed. Wild laughter rose, showers of crackling sparks that endlessly celebrated the raptor's demise. The little miscreants yelped in chorus, *She's kicked it! About time, too!* The phrases came whistling through the door to lodge in the heart of the screaming Lady and steal her breath away. She was dead for real, struck down by an unknown enemy who had silenced her domineering prattle. *Kicked it!* The little brood outside the door kept repeating the magic phrase with clacks of the tongue. *Kicked it.* Never had such a horror entered Grandmother's ears, she who had always taught those little ingrates to speak correctly, in French as in their native tongue. *Kicked it.* A cold tear leaked from beneath the inert eyelids. The mortified corpse didn't want anyone at her bedside anymore. And now the little demons, opening the door oh so gently, entered in single file. They stood at the foot of the bed, arms folded, heads bent, biting their lips; the moribund could clearly hear the phrase chime as it trotted around in their heads: *Kicked it! Kicked it!* They had stood there, not moving, not raising their eyes, trying to smother their helpless giggles. Then, slowly, heads bowed, they turned on their heels and exited the room in single file. Grandmother found herself alone once more, waiting for the cold to take her. In the living room, the mad laughter burst out again before drooping like soggy plumes. The brood, suddenly fallen silent, moved away on tiptoe. The outer door closed with a dull click on the deserted apartment. The little ones hurtled down the stairs. Quick, quick, outside, into the fresh air! *She's kicked it!* And ran to catch the last bus. And walked at top speed through the streets. Aimlessly. At night. In the cold. Coats flapping open, without a scarf. Hair all tangled. And jumped feet together into puddles to get their shoes wet, catch pneumonia, sneeze while cackling like overripe schoolgirls. And went into a packed, overheated dive, where the spoons and chopsticks were at the end of the table, jumbled together in a filthy container. And ordered sweet and sour soup for three, served in a steaming tureen set down in the middle of the grimy table. And greedily gulped down the fish and tamarind soup, Grandmother's favorite, as she lay all alone in her bed, where icy tongues lapped respectfully at her toes. It was hot in the dive, a heat laden with smells. The little miscreants had taken off their coats, which draped onto the floor. They poached vegetables out of the tureen, shredded the fish, seasoned their bowls of rice with generous spoonfuls of broth. The youngest, who was already the tallest, perched on her gorgeous gams, placed on the tip of her tongue a ring of hot pepper that she bit with a grimace. And the other two sputtered with laughter. They had even removed their sweaters and rolled up their shirtsleeves, the better to wipe their elbows on the grimy tabletop. And they jabbered, clucked with their mouths full, cheeks red, eyes shining. The oldest conducted herself a bit more properly than the other two. She couldn't help flicking her earlobes. The pearls were still there, like condor's eyes circling above the tureen, which was emptied in no time flat and was replaced in the middle of the table by fried coconut balls, Grandmother's favorite dessert, as she lay all alone in her bed, where icy tongues groomed her thighs in frozen silence. The little brood munched coconut balls and slurped tea and the chattering went on full blast. So much stuff and nonsense spouted in a single breath, lips on fire. Each pursued her own babble; spit sprayed joyously across the table. Lying in her bed, where the icy tongues were now planting their spikes in her stomach, the cadaver strained to hear the chattering of her brood. The little miscreants were not talking about Grandmother. They were blabbing in French, having completely forgotten the corpse, stiff with rage in her bed, where the icy suckers were pumping her blood. Of the three miscreants, only the eldest had a bit of a guilty conscience. She poked nervously at her earlobes—the condor's eye was still there, firmly attached. And, while the other two rattled on in French, now and then she piped up with a few chirps of her native warble, like a tribute to the imperious Lady. It quivered on the chairs, the sated bellies, the swollen lips, the crumbs of fried coconut clinging to their arms and even their hair. The little beasts were in no rush to go home. They had all night to yap away, flit about the streets, flap their arms like birds raised in a cage, a bit dazed by the wide-open sky. And to hop across the road, pressing their beaks against lit display windows. And to buy cigarettes for the first time, which they smoked while coughing and laughing like mad. Then they went to the station to watch the last trains pull out, reading in hushed, excited voices the names of distant cities on the departures board. Shivering, they took refuge in the waiting room, all three sitting very stiff, squeezed against each other, opposite a bearded old man who was dreaming aloud of dry sausage, lying on a bench, newspapers tied around his chest with a rope. They jumped up in a single movement when their eyelids grew heavy. And bought, with the last of their change, a can of beer from the vending machine in the departure lounge. And, making a face, each drank a single gulp. Then the half-empty can was abandoned at the station exit, posed quietly next to a silhouette buried under a mountain of rags. The little she-devils began to feel tired. They walked slowly, in single file, heads bowed. Their teeth chattered and their arms were crossed to hold shut the flaps of their coats. And they went, dragging their feet, up to the river, to see the color of the water at night, and stood just at the edge of the quay, bodies straining forward, the toes of their shoes making a beeline for the void. And they balanced along the quay in Indian file, arms spread, legs wobbling, like tightrope walkers in danger of being sucked down by the void and swallowed by the river. And they descended the stairs at the very end of the quay, climbed down the slippery steps to the lowest ones covered in moss, and stood there, feet in the frigid water. To top it off, the little nitwits took each other's hands, ready to let themselves sink like an impious rosary, certain that someone would fish them out only when the icy tongues had finished devouring Grandmother to the roots of her hair, and her sense-less remains had been removed from the bed and shoved below the earth. Then someone would fish all three of them out and give them a shot to the heart. They would cough up all the black water, scrape the green and mauve spots from their cheeks, start awake, and return to the bedroom—where, beneath the crucifix, there would be no more Grandmother muttering her prayers from morning till night, screaming in fury against the Commu-nists who had stolen everything from her, her old-style houses and stylish flunkies, villa with pool and Moi gardener, her huge sedan and pockmarked but faithful chauffeur, not to mention her funeral services, her hearses by the dozens, her wreaths by the thousands, her banquet caterers, her flamboyant village bands, her priests hired by the hour, her monks dispatched at a mo-ment's notice, and her army of ultra-chic pallbearers in their white uniforms with gold buttons, gallooned caps, and matching gloves. Once her steely tongue had decapitated the Red army, Grand-mother, out of breath but still shaking with rage, fell onto the other object of her wrath and thrust her skewer into King Lear, the layabout in his little blue house, who had sold his two daugh-ters for two precious statuettes. Grandmother could never let that story go. Because even the Crucified One above the bed had borne witness to the infamy. While she was in the blue house, plotting to snatch away the two orphans in the huge sedan wait-ing to hightail it out of Saigon, King Lear, taking advantage of a momentary lapse in attention, had rummaged through her alli-gator purse and swiped the two precious statuettes under the very eyes of the Crucified One, brought along in the selfsame purse as a talisman to protect the noble Lady from lynching by the rising and vociferous hordes of Communist riffraff. Grand-mother turned and turned King Lear's effigy on the spit of her rantings, but the skewered scoundrel eluded her grasp and thumbed his nose. Which didn't prevent Grandmother from conducting, day after day from her exiled bed, the trial of the Saigon swine, who had managed to stick her with these two orphans while he had it easy in his cozy little blue house. Sitting in her bed, basking in the aura of the Crucified One, Grandmother recited her litanies and her rosary. And just when you least expected it, a hail of imprecations against King Lear, screeched in shrill Vietnamese, tore through the threnody of Aves that she murmured in languid French. Then Lady Jackal regained her breath and crossed herself, still moving her lips like a squid that had spit out the last of its ink, knowing in her heart of hearts that her conversion was largely due to the theft of the two stone idols. Fleeing Saigon, Grandmother had shoved the two statuettes, the jade magot and the carved emerald Buddha, in her purse along with the crucifix. Two kinds of protector were better than one, when the earth trembled beneath a rich man's feet. The Buddha with his uproarious backside and prosperous belly had jumped ship before they even got out of the city. Whereas the other tutelary soldier, with his gaunt face, crown of thorns, and lanky torso, had stuck it out to the bitter end, safeguarding not only Lady Jackal's body and soul but also the diamonds stashed in her mouth, the gold crammed in the soles of her shoes, and the money belt that chafed her skin beneath her blouse. Learning from her misadventure, Grandmother in her exile now served only one master, the Crucified One hanging above her bed, whom she'd promoted to watchman over her dominion-cum-strongbox: for the hoarder had filled the tiniest crevice of her cave with sparkling stones and gold nuggets. At night, she locked herself in her room. The moment she awoke, she inspected her thirteen hiding places one by one, from the fake mothball that encased her most precious jewel to the old box of sticky candies with, in the middle, a faded pink wrapper enfolding a hard yellow treat, shaped like a signet ring, which you'd best not bite into unless you wanted to lose a tooth. Every morning, Lady Jackal verified all the hidey-holes containing her scattered treasure. Only then did she begin her toilette, having bolted the door to her lair behind her. The little miscreants were permitted to enter the chamber merely to make the bed, vacuum the floor, and dust the furniture and crucifix, under the watchful eye of the jackal who sat in a corner and never once let down her guard.

When the condor started flying low, she began dropping her diamonds one by one into the maw of the sly fox who showed up one day at the door of their big gloomy apartment to sell the banished one, the humiliated one, the dispossessed one a membership in the League for the Regeneration of Vietnam, a league of which the sly fox was president and sole active member. He appeared at the homes of the banished, humiliated, dispossessed (of whom he kept an electronic database), in his regalia as an officer of the former anti-Communist army, and pled on his feet (heart pounding with nostalgia beneath the row of medals and faded rosettes) for the extermination of the riffraff who had seized power and routed the army whose uniform he still wore. The sly fox, in a profusion of scraping bows and salutations, arrived at dinner time on the dot, which with a sigh of famished pride he consented (bow) to share, for the sole purpose of furthering (in grandiloquent French) the political edification of the little miscreants (accusatory index) whom the charitable, the heroic, the incomparable Lady (obsequious gesture) had rescued (bow) from the Communist hydra (gnashing of teeth), spiriting them to safety in her talons, on which the sly fox applied and reapplied his soft soap with the persistent humility (unctuous smile) of an ingratiator who knew how to anoint the tight-fisted with oil until the gold and sparklers fell from their claws. The gold, sparklers, and even rolls of banknotes dropped into the pocket of the sly fox, who, having gained a new lease on life, went off (heart pounding with nostalgia beneath the row of medals and faded rosettes) to sing elsewhere the praises of his League, and forgot about honoring with his scraping bows and salutations the dying Lady, who had kept for herself only her two pearls, and who died envisioning the statue that a regenerated Vietnam would erect to the memory of its savior, but frowning at the thought that the little miscreants no longer had anyone to remind them (index vibrating with authority) of their devotional obligations toward the incomparable Lady, who vowed to haunt them with her charitable specter. Brrr! My older cousin shivered, a hand on her belly, the other rubbing her arm—Grandmother's visitation had chilled her blood. I had picked up my book, abandoned by my younger cousin, who was wiping up the remains of the dead ant with a sprayed rag that she pushed energetically with her foot, while whistling a lively tune. She had tucked her hair behind her ears, revealing a suddenly joyful countenance and a mouth that puckered spiritedly, while she rocked her body from right to left and, with the tip of her bare foot, traced with the damp rag strokes and haloes on the tiling. The floorcloth twisted behind the chair where my older cousin was exposing herself to the afternoon sun. She kept one hand on her belly, while the other caressed a pearl-laden earlobe, those precious pearls bequeathed by the dying Lady. In return, my cousin had sworn to demand an accounting from the scoundrel at the earliest opportunity. So when King Lear was there, tucked in bed in the room destined for the child, she would come sit on the edge of the fold-out and wrest from the old man the confession of his former crime. Because after all, as the moribund had reiterated (taking the crucifix as witness), those two statuettes hadn't just walked off by themselves. The pockmarked chauffeur having been cleared after much rumination, the Lady's deep-seated conviction fell upon King Lear, who, with one and the same hand, had filched the loot and flicked away his progeny, sending them to find out if the air elsewhere smelled less of riff-raffery. And now, in that gleaming elsewhere, the progeny was preparing to welcome King Lear for a little tour of the well-scrubbed paradise. After which, with a snap, she would shoot the visitor back to his blue house, where the scent of flowers could barely cover the odor of indigence. But before re-expediting the old scoundrel, my cousins would lead him by the harness into the Caudine Forks that Grandmother had erected. No escaping it.

The eye of the charitable Lady was watching, demanding to be present for the outcome. The trap was set. King Lear was not exactly rushing headlong into the snare, but he was coming all the same, enticed by the aroma of reunions and the shimmer of the spanking new house, which in a blink would change into an interrogation chamber. They would tickle the old pirate's feet until he confessed to making off with the potbellied Buddha. Day and night they would harangue the old prevaricator, who claimed abandonment when it was he who had abandoned his progeny to the jackal's maw at the first little push. My cousin massaged her neck. The jackal released her but had left her mark. Every now and then, she was seized by the collar and yanked backward, into the bedroom where Grandmother pummeled King Lear with her crucifix before mashing him to a pulp. It was especially at night that the jackal's ghost came out to howl, around the bed where my cousin, burdened by her own mass, tossed and turned like a rudderless hot air balloon, trying to land on the solid ground of sleep—which the nutsandbolts man lying next to her had reached in one mellow bound, judging by the regular whistles that rose from behind the broad back made of chalk and sand and bricks of Germanic good sense, burnished with a light Tibetan patina. At night, when the jackal's howling etched her eardrums, my cousin huddled under the comforter. She rested her head against the brick wall and, eyes wide open in the dark, listened to the sleeper's peaceful wheezing. Now and then the wheezing stopped short and the dreamer fidgeted, horrified at having forgotten the grand lama's visit or at losing his way to the prayer center. These pangs of conscience left nary a scratch on the wall built of chalk and sand. The sleeper retreated behind his fortified rampart and the whistling resumed. Her head butting the wall, rocked by the calm wheeze that had silenced the screech of the ghost demanding her nest egg, my cousin sometimes managed to catch a sleep train. But most of the time she watched them glide by, eyes wide open in the dark, wondering what she had ever seen in that wall, how many hundreds of nights she would still be listening to the wheezing rise from behind it. The wall could handle any chore, no doubt about it, but did one marry a wall, even one built of chalk and sand? And, in bed, a wall, even coated in Tibetan wisdom, didn't exactly make you break out in a sweat. It was all of a piece, clean and angular. It didn't stink of vice, musk, lustful spit, lecherous spunk; it smelled nice, like vegetable soap and lavender detergent. It laid itself over you, didn't tickle you anywhere, rubbed against you, bruised your pelvic bone, shuddered a bit, and then it was done. The bricks of Germanic good sense were only good at refrigerating your heart, not to mention the rest of you. Otherwise, they were so solid, so airtight, that you could take refuge behind them, beat your head against them, let out a prolonged sob: the wall never shook, never wavered. As if it never heard you heave those sighs, toss and turn like that, huddle beneath the quilt to hide from the phantom howling at the foot of the bed. As if this solid wall were simply obtuse. As if you could die of fright there, behind the wall, and it wouldn't even hear you drop. As if the specters of the past could shove you there, against the wall, and train their rifles on you; the rampart would not even feel the ghostly bullets as they tore through your flesh. As if it really were a wall, which wheezed at night to rock you to sleep, and that was all. You could try gluing your ear to it hoping to hear something new, but nothing doing! You could try prodding it, but it wouldn't budge. You could try scratching it the way someone buried alive claws at the lid of her coffin, it wouldn't cede an inch of ground. You could beat against it with your fists, it wouldn't open. And yet it was such sturdy material to have in one's home, strapping and rock solid, made to resist invasion by cockroaches and assault by ghosts. A wall turned toward the future, the light, the sun; but on the other side of the rampart, when you lay your head against it at night, it felt cold. A deathly chill. The chill of a shared tomb, when one is asleep and the other, not; when one is whistling like a kettle that has had its fill and the other's wide-open peepers burn with insomnia; when one stretches out over his bit of territory and the other tosses and turns in her eternal plot. My cousin drove herself crazy trying to enflame the wall. But the bricks of Germanic good sense were made only to hold up the new house, sparkling kitchen, and nursery wallpapered with pink elephants—the complete arsenal of happiness, which my cousin had always wanted to take by storm, like a good little soldier who enjoyed marching in step, never veered onto side paths, and, while on night watch in the eternal plot, barely allowed herself to dream just a little bit, about everything she had tried before the wall was built, before the back made of chalk and sand had blocked out the sun. For while waiting for the demigod who would devote his little barb to her alone, the brazen hussy had flailed like a regular banshee, jumped one joker after another, scraped every string with her bow, learned the guitar in ten easy lessons, danced the jig, bought a drum that went chica-boom, ordered paint sets, set up an easel, bought a box that went click-clack, designed dresses, bought a machine that went zigzag, nursed dwarf trees, bought a miniature fountain that went splish-splash, crammed basic Japanese easy-peasy, mimicked the art of tea, bought a rare tea service financed in a hugger-mugger, but try as she might to go clickclackchicaboomzigzag, the days went by willy-nilly, the detritus of failed vocations piled up pell-mell, and it was always the same bric-a-brac of boredom that found itself waiting for the fortuitous smish-smash of a savior who burst in lickety-split to cure these fits and untangle this mish-mash of whim-whams. Said whim-whams had spun my cousin's head round and round, emptied her pockets, left her still yearning to stock her little boutique with an extra measure of heart. The savior who fell from heaven reached under the detritus of failed vocations and pulled out a lost soul eager to be branded, to sell off her cart-load of whim-whams, swap the extra measure of heart for a gleaming kitchen, trade in the boxes that went clickclackchicaboom for a mewling blob of jelly that went waah waah at any hour of the day or night. For in all her zigzagging, the lost soul had forgotten the tick-tock of age. While she was frolicking, time had pursued its game of tic-tac-toe. And once the clickclackchicaboom was over and done, the clock began tick-tocking something fierce in the whim-wham graveyard. The savior dropped in just in time to pluck the ripe fruit. The green was turning mauve. The pink was getting dusky. The bell was tolling for her youth, drowning out the caterwaul of strings fiddled a-go-go. Her whim-whams now stowed in the attic, the lost soul devoted her life to the savior who had dropped into her bed, calm block here fallen from a celestial joy. A flawless brick, all smooth, square, and dry, the heart of the wall, which had reared up without warning, blocking out the sun. But behind the wall, the lost soul had her spanking new enclosure, bricks of good sense on which to lay her head and, soon, a demigod who would go waah waah then clickclackchicaboomsplish-splash, carving out his own little slice of heart before getting his own spanking new enclosure and, inside it, a mewling demigod who'd go waah waah before sounding all the bells and whistles. All super-duper and hunky-dory, everything ship-shape. Until the demigod gets his head caught in the wringer—and then wham bam! No more flim-flam. From then on, the demigod's only option was to listen to the tick-tock of eternity beneath a layer of humus. Humus was precisely what the spanking new house needed. Good, rich fertilizer to nourish the little flower of sensory pleasures that was about to give out and take a nosedive. The flower of sensory pleasures grew as best it could in the bed of arid fancy. Even the garden of delights looked more like a vegetable plot, clean and tidy, just barely containing a few strictly necessary plants. Sitting in her new enclosure, my cousin tried to turn a deaf ear, but every morning she heard the clank of deadbolts in her prison, followed by the plip-plop of boredom distilled drip by drop. In this yawning void waiting to welcome the cry of the other savior, the aye! aye! of the little angel who, for now, beat a silent drum, kicking against the walls of his cave, my cousin came and went, unable to thread her way through the droplets dripping from the ceiling, where her interminable sighs had deposited a thick coating of lassitude. To dissipate these condensed clouds, the prisoner ate, cooked then ate, ate then cooked, in a tête-à-tête with her little radio, when she wasn't spitting out chicabooms beneath the high-performance range hood that vacuumed in cooking odors but couldn't suck up the wafts of ennui. No two ways around it, it's all my cousin thought about: Cooking and eating. Eating and cooking. Dishes that called upon her best efforts. Heavy, oily, spicy dishes that gave off clouds of steam, weighed heavily on your tongue and stomach, warmed your belly, trundled gurgles up and down your drainpipe, rattled your foundations. My cousin ate slowly, taking her time, the only captain of this ship, where the radio squawked without managing to silence the flurry of jim-jams in her head. So then she choked off the braying voice tallying up the dead from the far corners of the globe, the corpses of the luckless who didn't even console her for her melancholy. And in the silence of her enclosure, she sniffed the odor of rösti done to a turn, while listening to herself chew the meat smothered in thick brown sauce. Recipe books piled up in the cabinet. When she had finished eating and cooking, cooking and eating, my cousin would snap up one of those codices, which she lay before her on the large gleaming table. Brows knit, gustatory antennae on the alert, tongue flicking over the edge of her lips, she turned the pages, watching for the mind-boggling recipe, the drastic remedy for boredom, which she could prescribe for herself and then administer to King Lear, when he came to fill a bit of this yawning void. This called for a dish to end all dishes, something to enflame the taste buds of the old man who had also begun cooking things up in the rear courtyard of the blue house, which on a whim he'd fashioned into an outdoor kitchen.

↓

He cooked over hot coals. Dishes he adapted the way he grew his flowers, mixing ingredients as he pleased. He spent all morning in the rear court, eyes tearing, nose stung by the smoke, tending the embers, grinding spices, grilling eels, pluming poultry. Saigon was well stocked since the airplanes started dropping saprophytes onto the city, King Lear said in his letters. He went to market bright and early, when his rusty joints didn't hurt so much. He walked slowly, with his friend the priest who had only a reedy thread of voice left (words struggled to emerge from his lips, his ravaged face contorted with the effort, the gray, collapsed veins in his neck swelled, his mouth formed the words but the sound was rasping). King Lear walked with his head bent to the side, ear tendered toward that voice, cracked from having screamed in terror for nights on end at the bottom of his damp hole, his only reply the shrieks of the watchful rats huddled in a corner where the moon never shone. The two old men spent much of their time at the market, looking and choosing, letting themselves be pushed along by the masses. The priest's tall stature made him stand out from the crowd, but his legs had weakened in the damp pit. Occasionally he had to lean on King Lear's arm. He clutched onto his friend and his eyes peered around in terror, as during those moonlit nights when the rats ventured into the damp hole. He stood petrified a moment, then straightened up, let go of King Lear, and his silhouette again drifted through the crowd. From a distance, one would have seen a pike with a puppet's face jammed on the end, a slightly comical death's head, with white hair, a gentle gaze, and a simulacrum of voice that was lost in the hubbub. Returning home, the two friends took a walk around the little garden of the blue house. The flowers pressed against each other like crowds at the market. The sun was already high when they went into the rear courtyard. King Lear busied himself around the fire. The priest sat in a corner. They spoke little—about the freshness of the food or the seeds and bulbs that had just arrived in a small package, sent by his elder daughter. King Lear dreamed of digging a pond in the middle of the flowers. A little mosquito mirror. A puddle where he would raise eels and draw enough water for his flowers. The priest sat upright in his chair, hands on his knees. He watched the smoke rise heavenward, into a limpid sky barely scratched by a trace of mist. A pure sky, which had never seen bodies huddled in damp pits. A tranquil sky, which had never shuddered at hearing screams of terror rising from the abyss. An impenetrable sky, which had never lowered the ladder of mercy toward hands straining from the depths of black holes. The priest's eyes followed the smoke as it dissipated and slowly expired beneath the blue vellum. Just like my voice, the priest said to King Lear. My strangled voice. My voice that scraped out words, no longer screamed, no longer begged, no longer sang, no longer prayed, no longer asked for anything from the Butcher on high who sliced supplicants' vocal cords and cut the tendons of the insubordinate. The Wheezer, as King Lear called him in his letters, the Wheezer no longer said mass, but he had a room of his own at the church. A dark little room, furnished with this and that. A table, two chairs, an armchair, a bed behind a screen, the trinkets of devotion on the wall and, beneath them, the Wheezer sitting all day long in his chair, doing his martyr routine for the faithful who came to see the saint, touch the saint, receive rasping sounds from the mouth of the saint. A real sideshow, said the Wheezer. And I'm the main attraction. Sitting there like some heavenly derelict, wooden bowl on the table, halo perfectly adjusted, mimicking devotion for the poor, intimidated faithful, their fists in their pockets squeezing wadded-up banknotes, hardly daring lift their eyes to the martyr. They cross themselves. They'd like to kiss my hand, fall at my knees, wash my feet. They drop their wadded-up bills into the bowl. They're ashamed at having only this to offer the saint. Their eyes well up when they hear me wheeze. I make as if to stand. They panic, protest, force me to sit back down. They gently touch the body of the saint. The body that the Communists couldn't break. The valiant carcass, beaten, chained, tossed into the damp pit, and that came back, mangled, crawling, to sit among knickknacks of the faith. They believe I'm on a par with the Son of the Butcher. They believe I let myself be flayed alive out of love for the Dismemberer, sitting atop his carnage, picking his teeth with the splinters of the innocent. They believe I cracked my voice so as not to renounce Him. They believe that in my damp pit I prayed and that my prayer dried my blood, abated my hunger, splinted my dislocated bones. But in the depths of my hole, I was screaming in terror. I called out to the Great Deaf-Mute. So that He might yank me out of there. So that He would snatch me away from those miscreant swine, the political commissars and their howling flunkies. I screamed. The howling flunkies pistol-whipped me. I screamed. They shoved my head into their latrines. I screamed. They scalded my back. I screamed. They came with shears to cut off my tongue, but in the end they didn't. They were afraid of the Great Deaf-Mute, who might hear the squeaking of shears and punish them. They let me keep it. I went on screaming. The Great Deaf-Mute didn't turn a hair, concealed behind his blue screen, spying on the sight of his puppets flailing on the slippery slope, wallowing in hemoglobin under a makeshift big top, until a hand grabbed them by the scruff of the neck and tossed them outside, into the dark. Since the Communists had grabbed him, the Wheezer's head was no longer on quite straight. *Since he had been reeducated,* King Lear wrote in his letters to flatter the censor's eye, which might reawaken at the slightest pinprick and send King Lear for some reeducation of his own. The Wheezer said nothing for hours on end. Then, all at once, his reedy voice cranked up and you couldn't make him stop. He shot poisoned arrows at the blue vellum and the arrows rained back down on his head. He spat into the wind and the wind whipped the gob back in his face. He shook his fist in the air and a bird shat on his skull. He called to the Great Deaf-Mute and only King Lear listened, with a weary ear, grilling eels that he then set on the table, on a plate between two bottles of beer. Grilled eels were all that could mollify the Wheezer. He sniffed the scent of eel flesh browned to perfection and forgot all about cursing the Butcher on high. He chewed slowly. Half his teeth had been spit out at the feet of the howling flunkies. The few sharpened fangs still left him he nursed for the day when he would bite the Great Deaf-Mute in the thick of his shank. The slices of eel melted in your mouth. Until they were all swallowed, he said nothing. King Lear watched him empty the plate, while nibbling at a small slice of those eels prepared specially for the Wheezer. Eels cut in strips and cooked plain, or sliced into rings, stuffed with herbs, and grilled. The chef varied the recipe, rationed the amount. Never a slice too many. Just enough to stoke your appetite and leave the back of your throat wanting a bit more, so that the Wheezer could dream about them afterward, sitting in his sideshow stall and waiting for his flock to arrive. Dreaming of eels, of the aroma of grilled eels, was enough to put him in ecstasy. He wanted no other beatitude, jibbed at any other rapture. The incense of the faith had stopped turning his head a long time ago. And he had to give them their money's worth, those poor lambs who had shorn themselves, bled themselves dry so they could bring something when they came bleating around the sacrificial one. The sacrificial one rested his pious gaze on them, but what his eyes saw were long, viscous tubes that King Lear grasped, swatted, cut into sections, speared on a small skewer, and turned over and over above the open flame. The Wheezer's eyes shone as he sat in the darkness of his hovel. He was tickled to death at the trick he'd pulled on the exalted Tease. It was over. He had battened the hatches. The exalted Tease could send as many sirens as he wanted to wail at the porthole; the only thing he listened to now was his gut. He still played at being a fisherman, just to hold onto his little corner in the house of the Great Deaf-Mute, who owed him that much at least. His whines and wheezes were highly prized among the faithful. In several months, he had already harvested enough to restore the church façade.

He'd also have to refurbish the interior. The political commissars had ended up yanking the martyrs from their putrid holes and sending them back to the church, their orchestra pit, but it was an awfully bare auditorium in which the revenants played their celestial arrangements. The sacramental knickknacks, swiped. The ecclesiastical furbelows, gone. The howling flunkies had made away with the whole décor. Of course, there were forms they could file with the police to recover their trinkets. Might as well spit in an empty well. And since the international airplanes had started excreting saprophytes onto the city, Saigon was now full of sparkling thuribles, ciboria whose silver didn't flake, duty-free candles and freshly copied altarpieces. The Wheezer aimed to thumb his nose at the blue vellum, repay evil with good, mount a spiritual con game to furnish the Tease's litter, offer Him a well-scrubbed cocoon, stuffed to bursting with all the latest knickknacks. Including a flock of sheep shorn bare, led by a stentor in saint's furbelows. All those zeroes bleating in chorus in the fully renovated cottage that awaited only its lessor; but the Great Deaf-Mute was too busy squatting on carnage steaming with blood. The fervent clamor of the shorn barely tickled his ear hairs. Still, the Wheezer hadn't skimped on the furnishings. The mike was top of the line. The speakers had never been used. The stentor recited himself hoarse. In the four corners of the church, the loudspeaker asked *Miserere mei deus,* and the chorus of the shorn repeated *Miserere.* But the Great Deaf-Mute might well pinch his nose, jerk his head from side to side: his ears remained stopped up. He heard only a continuous buzzing from below, swelling the blue vellum. Luckily, that was some tough material he had beneath his feet; it had never ripped, not even under intense pressure. The Great Deaf-Mute was at peace. He trundled about from slaughterhouse to slaughterhouse. There was always another one to inspect. And there, at least, no one was bleating. He could sit for days on the same heap of bones and carrion, filling his nostrils with the reeking silence. The Wheezer was perfectly aware of this. He had seen the slaughterhouse Inspector lean over his damp pit, sniff, and move on because it smelled like rage and discontent in there, and death hadn't yet flown down with its xyster. The Wheezer lost his voice that night, when he saw the Inspector turn away from the rotten hole where he was shivering with fever. Now that he was well out of it, he assumed his own lordly manner. He cashed in on his wispy voice and bent martyr's back, if for no other reason than to offer a lovely furnished cage to the Great Deaf-Mute, who only had to lift the lid—the bleating of His flock would rise to the blue vellum, just like the smoke of grilled eels. The Wheezer always came back to that, to the smell of those sea serpents stuffed with herbs and browned over open coals. He was unhappy like an eel under the cleaver whenever King Lear snuck off to see the ocean. The traitor always departed without warning, catching the early bus, and the Wheezer, who would show up all expectant at the blue house, was left high and dry. So he watered the flowers in the garden, listlessly, just to show King Lear there were no hard feelings. Though in the back of his mind was the thought that if his friend was pleased with the flowers when he got back, it might spur him on culinarily. He might even devise a new eel recipe, though the diner was of the conviction that nothing beat eels plain grilled. Days passed and still King Lear did not return. The Wheezer came every morning. He watered the flowers. He went to the market and let his bones be jostled by the crowd. The rest of the day he meandered about the streets. Sometimes he let himself be carted to the river in a Honda taxi. He wandered along the banks, sad as a sliced eel. There were plenty of spots where people could order his sea serpent. A restaurant on the river, with swingy music and imported Chinese lanterns, even featured seven different ways of enjoying eels. The Wheezer had gone there once to partake of the seven eely sins. It had cost him the equivalent of three dozen Bibles. The eels were frozen. They tasted like papier-mâché, like the hosts they shoved down the throats of the worshipers at his church. King Lear finally returned from Vung

Tau, bringing with him some nice plump eels. Happy days were here again. There was smoke in the rear court. The beer was cold, the eel flesh as delicate as could be. The Wheezer, refreshed after his treat, went back to the church and performed like a pro, though with a sense of dread that his cook might abandon him for a long spell. A letter had arrived. King Lear had put on his glasses, read all that prose with a placid eye. Then he had slid the letter back into its envelope and fanned the coals with it. The Wheezer couldn't smoke anything out of him. But barely were they at the table when King Lear mentioned, casual as you please, that he wouldn't mind hopping halfway across the world to pay his princesses a little visit. The Wheezer nearly choked on his eel. It had been twenty years since they'd scampered off after their grandmother, who'd orchestrated funerals for the stinking rich. They had abandoned him there, in the blue house, just as the Communists were entering the city. And now they whistled and he, the good slob, was at their beck and call. More of the Great Deaf-Mute's mischief. But the Wheezer kept his venomous thoughts to himself. To King Lear, he only nodded. Then silence fell and they emptied the plate as usual, without a word. The Wheezer hoped and prayed that he'd hear no more about this. The little escapades to Vung Tau were hard enough to swallow. Since he had received the letter, King Lear didn't stay as long at the seashore. At first the Wheezer had taken it as a sign of repentance, but then the cook lifted the scales from the diner's eyes. The truth was, King Lear used to go to Vung Tau like a lover on a pilgrimage, to stare at the ocean where his little ones had set sail. The letter's arrival had changed all that. The old crank had recovered his senses, and from now on he would take better care of himself. Now he went to Vung Tau to keep in shape, fill his lungs with fresh air, and stretch his joints. Still more of the Great Deaf-Mute's mischief. Something you had to swallow whole, like raw eel. You had to see King Lear, all pumped up like an athlete, arms and legs flailing about amid the flowers. Eyes sparkling, with the beatific expression of someone who still thought he was full of vim and vigor, he got up with the soup merchant, went to the door to breathe in the air squeezed between the high-rise sapro-phytes flanking his decrepit palace, and, his lungs filled with the stench of haphazardly dug sewers, the reborn youngster made his cadaverous hinges creak. The flowers were still laughing at that one. The grilled eels, too. The postmortem hilarity tickled the Wheezer's guts, and he could barely suppress a ventriloquial guf-faw. King Lear noticed none of this. Fitness mania had gripped him and would not let go. Every day the fever rose higher. He ate vegetables, stopped drinking beer, talked to his flowers, and rubbed down his legs with miracle ointment bought at the market for a few cents. King Lear shored up his ruins, planed his rough edges, shined his pelt, cleansed his viscera; he acted casual, but was dis-ciplined and meticulous like a champion before the big jump — worse, a disjointed bridegroom refurbished for the occasion. For what the Wheezer was seeing amounted to wedding preparations. Next, the escapees' fiancé would go rummaging in his closet for the suit tailor-made by the most famous cloth-cutter in Saigon. King Lear was fond of such get-ups. His friend had seen him lin-ger at the new haberdashers' windows. He gauged the merchan-dise with a connoisseur's eye and scornful pout. All those mod-els shabbily cut in local workshops were fit only for rubes. King Lear had turned over and over the question of how to drape his skeleton. Then he'd presented himself to the best ragman around. One week later, arriving at the blue house, the Wheezer had come nose to nose with a chi-chi wreck, a dog-eared fashion plate, re-fined and melancholy like Ha Long Bay on the sepia postcards they sold to unsuspecting tourists. But even back then, the Wheezer was keeping his poisonous opinions to himself. King Lear had started brushing off his finery the minute he'd got wind of his el-der daughter's nuptials. He wanted to be ready and waiting for the feast. But the princesses hadn't whistled that time, and he, the good slob, had hung his accoutrements back in the closet without a word.

I'd laid a stack of cookbooks at my cousin's feet, which she leafed through distractedly. She'd surely end up laying her hands on King Lear's letter. A tiny little letter, hardly bigger than a prescription slip and scarcely more legible. She was certain she'd pressed it in one of her codices. She always slid King Lear's letters into her cooking manuals, to keep them in sight for a few days, long enough to mark them with a greasy border; after that, they were good only for scooping up peelings. In any case, even studying them with a magnifying glass, my cousin had never found anything to stop her in her tracks, keep her so spellbound she burned her latest recipe. All the same, this time, the scribbler might have put himself out just a bit. This wasn't just some grub she was cooking up, but a full-blown commemorative banquet. An out-and-out feast offered to the old man, who must not have had a single pinch of emotion to put on his tongue in years. And she was preparing him something to satisfy his craving for love, enflame his deserted palate, make his ticker dance just as it was winding down. My cousin mumbled her complaints while flipping the pages of a large notebook crawling with her rounded handwriting, like a swarm of chubby ants fleeing a bath of blue dye. This was her personal pharmacopoeia, her provision of emetics, her exotic antidotes, her recipes from the old country, applied only sparingly, like cataplasms on little burns of nostalgia. When the heavy, spiced dishes no longer soothed her fits of boredom, my cousin opened her grimoire and made herself medicinal preparations, exactly as Grandmother had taught her and according to the formulas she had consigned to her secret codex. Which she now turned this way and that, shook and tapped—in vain. It refused to cough up the letter, the same as the books spread at my cousin's feet. And yet she was almost sure now of having left King Lear's prose to marinate at the page of pig's ears in vinaigrette. She could still remember the little slivers of ear that she mashed between her teeth while reading the letter. She had even told herself she'd have to surprise the old man with those little porcine ears, deliciously crunchy and coated in good, spicy vinaigrette. Grandmother had adored them, but she didn't have the teeth for them, so she'd watched my cousin crunch those earlets that she'd taught her how to scrape clean of hair, slice, cook, then marinate in richly spiced and flavored oil. King Lear's letter was not stuck between the pages for pork in vinaigrette. Nor was it with the bird's nest soup, a royal concoction never prepared, consigned to the notebook once upon a time with the ulterior motive of administering a princely dose on her wedding day. But she hadn't counted on the Swiss desiderata of the Lamaist, who prescribed for the nuptials a palate cleanser of buttered tea, followed by a few mouthfuls of Tibetan sagacity. The prescription mainly called for a cure by game animals, an analeptic of melted cheeses, washed down by cream- and wine-based potions. And after all that, my cousin was left wanting. She had not been allowed to open her grimoire and prepare her secret formula for the big day, but still she didn't concede defeat. She would make King Lear swallow what she hadn't been able to feed the meditator—who demanded horse remedies for his constitution and his wall built of chalk and sand, and certainly not those little embroideries for sparrows, no heavier than a thimbleful of water and costing an arm and a leg. These accountings made the meditator's head spin. He felt funny spending, for three strands of algae filched from a swift, enough to stock a gold shipment's worth of cow's milk. Fie on lacy fineries for finicky palates and pursed lips! He had put a stop to all that nonsense. On the day of their wedding reception, which was held in an authentic Norman inn, molten gold had flowed from every place setting, into every mouth, before settling with all its ponderous weight in the swollen paunches seated around the table. Among these was the belly of Theo, festooned with banderillas freshly planted by my younger cousin, seated to his right and looking daggers at him, her own waist cinctured by a flamboyant skirt. High on his pleasure at being *with the family,* as he declaimed to the assembly, Theo hardly felt the banderillas with which my cousin was hoping to stem his verbal flow—three draughts of molten gold having obliterated his lessons in conduct and drowned out her admonitions. Theo ignored the irritated looks from his banderillera, absorbed kicks under the table without missing a beat. The engine was running full tilt, and now nothing could stop his gums from flapping. And in the midst of the nuptial hubbub, Theo, his mouth brimming with gold, launched into a panegyric of the great man he was preparing to become. They shouldn't put stock in appearances: his beaten dog's eyes, thug-like face, ragtag feathers, guzzling mouth, hands that didn't know what to do with themselves, and stained fingers cautiously keeping away from my cousin in the bright red skirt—who, now transformed into a dragon, blasted him with a sidelong glare, hissing through clenched teeth for him to pick up his fallen napkin, go wash his hands, and shut his big trap before the guests caught on to him—the guests who, he reiterated, should not put stock in his mangy exterior. He might look like a dish of tripe left out too long on a cafeteria counter, but in truth he was a great man in gestation, who had more than one trick and loads of beautiful people up the ratty sleeve of his flannel jacket—pocked as it might be with indelible stains that the flame-tailed dragon presently seated at his right had tried to lift, grumbling all the while, with a handkerchief moistened with spot remover. No detergent could get the better of the great man, who was not shy about displaying, like a seal of excellence, his aversion to washing. Appearances always counted against great men, Theo informed the guests, who were reveling in pheasant while emitting little *ohs* and *hmms.* Theo's words struck the wall of chitchat and fell like spent bullets, then rolled sadly back to sender, who, intoxicated by a mouthful of bleeding deer, immediately shot back a stream of circumlocutions that writhed in the air, seeking an emergency landing with a little traction. They ended up shrinking into themselves and dropping to the ground, flaccid and frustrated, like cranberry jelly on the plates of venison. After which, the triumphant chitchat drowned out the deer-eater's filibuster and turned the flood of words against him—those words that had formerly thrilled my pretty young cousin, once all ears but now transformed into a dragon, scarlet with rage, spitting a flame to consume the motormouth on the spot. The latter, dodging the breaths of the ignivomous dragon, continued to sculpt the statue of his greatness, painstakingly erecting it before the mocking eyes of the celebrants, who nodded their heads, opened their gobs, clucked their tongues, and downed every other boast with a forkful of doe and a swig of Graves, while awaiting their chance to get a word in and color themselves idols in turn. But nothing could top Theo's prolix offensive. And, each time he lifted his face from his still life with venison, the assembly received a volley smack in the kisser. Pell-mell, Theo's trap spewed famous names with whom he was all chummy-chummy and mind-boggling figures that could make a one-armed bandit spring its hinges. With a side dish of tentacular relations that could send an octopus jumping into the frying pan. To go with that, a fricassee of sharp operators, who unfortunately had fallen out with each other just when Theo went to seal the deal. And to top it off, a hodgepodge of penniless adventurers and gutless wonders with plenty to fall back on. It would have been the concoction of the century, if things hadn't turned sour just when Theo decided to stick his finger in the broth for a little taste. The pipeline was busted. The setback had completely wiped him out. Which was why the great man stood before them in such a down-and-out guise. But patience! Theo had more than one trick in his bag. One day he'd bounce back and, quick as a flash, go perch at the very top of the pyramid, where he would bask in the shade of his finally recompensed excellence, repelling with the tip of his loafer the shabby little creatures who tried to hike themselves up onto the royal platform. Shabby little creatures, incidentally, much like the face-stuffers currently seated level with the great man, who generously considered them, again incidentally, his supporting actors. Said actors were too stuffed to break any climbing records, not even to be crowned king of the stepstool. The pyramid didn't mean anything in particular to the assembly, who if they had their druthers would rather roll under the table than let the motor-mouth gum up their ear canals with his half-baked schemes. But— reveler's honor!—they would cling to that tablecloth as if it were the horizon line, with their ruddy, hiccupping moons floating above it. Playing on the acquiescent drowsiness of his support-ing cast, Theo the star, himself called to order by a violent ankle boot to his shin, climbed back down from his pyramidal dream to hike up my cousin in the red skirt. The pharaoh trained the spotlights on his darling, hoping that by giving her some of the applause he would mollify the dragon and make her stop send-ing him to the bathroom every five minutes to wipe the corner of his mouth, comb his greasy feathers, rinse the filaments of deer off his choppers, or remove that suspect new stain from the front of his jacket, which now had every attribute of a butcher's apron, including the smell—and the pharaoh did as he was told, with a wink at the audience. It was just a little game between the doll and her swain, who sometimes enjoyed playing the little doggy dragged along by his leash. At every hiss, Theo immediately stood up with a forced, magnanimous laugh. All the way to the rest-room, his jaw was clamped, his fist clenched in his pocket. He staggered to the sink, where he could shake that fist at his reflec-tion and stick out his coated tongue at the pathetic idiots sitting around the table in there, who took him for just a nice little doggy willing to sink to any depths to fetch his tasty treat under the red skirt. But of tasty treats, there had been none for months. The dé-cor of the love nest had changed. Now it was a Punch and Judy set. Just coughing or clearing his throat earned a whack from the nightstick. How quickly dolls turned into cops, or washroom attendants—just unbelievable. At first they ate out of your hand, and if it was cruddy they licked it clean for you. They glued themselves to your sweat. Your stench was their potpourri. Your stains they counted one by one, giddy like a teenage boy counting the freckles on a nudie poster. And if your hide shunned water, they rubbed their skin against you, massaged with soft almond milk. But once they'd sniffed out the whole story, caught that musty odor about you, like an old man molting in his corner, that was the end of the aroma fest. The slightest exhalation and they jerked open the windows. You shrank to the edge of the futon. Even your pores didn't dare breathe. One little sigh and you got a stake in your jugular. Dolls had no qualms about telling you you stank like a dead dog. No choice but to let yourself get shampooed like a circus poodle. And dolls kept their eye on you, like washroom attendants. They were there, always on the watch, sniffing your carcass and sending you back to the showers. Theo rinsed this bitterness from his mouth, rubbed his scummy teeth, flattened his feathers with the comb that the red-skirted cop had slipped authoritatively into his pocket. One last gander at the great man, who didn't look like much in the neon-lit mirror, and Theo cranked up his blarney machine, which charged ahead with brights on, bound and determined to dazzle the assembly. But back in the dining room, the red, doddering moons were no longer conferring over remains of venison: the revelers, while waiting for the wedding cake, had deserted the feast and taken their sated humors into the foyer, where buffet tables buckled under painted dishes and pewter steins. The loudspeakers emitted a hissing aria, soon drowned out by a fusillade of chicabooms, which a self-appointed discobolus, having slipped backstage to see to the hi-fi, threw into the foyer—making the dishes rattle and Theo's blood boil. Overtaken in the race to be life of the party, he found himself relegated to the pack of bit players, biding his time with a bottle of Veuve Cliquot in hand. Eye grim, wrathful lips barely appeased by the frothy widow, through his glass he watched the ruddy moons writhe amid the bubbles, imitating the steins crushed together on the buffet table, dancing and bumping into each other and holding each other by the handles. Even Baby had dived into the spawning pond. Her red skirt bobbed like a little goldfish skipping on the bubbles that spilled from the flute pitching between Theo's fingers. He leaned against the wall, gripping his magnum, and poured himself generous glassfuls. Downing the frothy head in huge gulps, he thought he could swallow all those writhing minnows. But one of them refused to follow the chain of bubbles, and the more he drank, the more Theo saw the small fry wiggling around his fairy-fish, who flew her scarlet flag with its siren's tail to bewitch a dozen fried and refried minnows that could barely make carp eyes at her. The gorgeous gams, rising from the foam, stretched longer by the minute; the red flag, tethered to its black-sheathed pole, flapped to the beat. A swing of the hip here, a thrust of the belly there. And the quartet of disheveled toadies reached out their hands to clutch onto her dragnet. She was playing the heartbreaker, right under Theo's nose, which got further bent out of joint and blocked his enjoyment of the widow—who, by tickling his tongue and gurgling in his gut, had helped him reset his fuses and relight his neon sign, a big blinking grin to reassure the crowd that, good sport that he was, he could take the joke of being temporarily consigned to the scrap heap. But he hadn't counted on Baby's maneuvers. In the blink of an eye, the undulations of the red skirt brushed away the widow's blandishments and Theo's forehead went scarlet; his neon sign flickered out. The command-performance grin trembled, turned into a rictus, then imploded like a blown lightbulb in a mute snicker. Before him, in the spawning ground, effervescence still ruled the day. The goldfish wiggled her little tail off, tightly surrounded by a school of guppies that wiped beads of sweat from their clammy skin while bopping their big heads to the boom-boom rhythm of the loudspeakers. And no one mourned the fact that Theo had shut down. The iron curtain had dropped with a thud and now the great man stood near the buffet, dignified as a defeated general over whose head the speakers fired their cannonade. He pulled his toga over his injuries, salved his wounds with the widow's remaining tears, and, when the magnum was empty, took his black gaze and rage-swollen lip to every corner of the room, in search of a flask still containing some elixir. But he found only the corpses of widows sucked to the last drop and, near the entrance, the immobile body of Southpaw. He'd forgotten about that one, "the cripple that once flew," as he called her, "the Albatrocious," the bird of ill omen *exiled on earth, amid the jeering crowd.* Glued to that piece of white wall, she looked like a stuffed bird of ill omen, placed there on watch. The only thing missing was the psychopathic taxidermist with Coke-bottle glasses, eczematous pincers, and whiny voice. The disgraced general left his dried-up widow on a sill and approached the forgotten sentinel. She stood stiffly, eyes riveted to the exit door, no doubt pondering some bit of merriment, like a squad of deranged killers bursting into the authentic Norman inn and thoroughly eviscerating all those wiggling fish. The general would have liked nothing better than to see that. He was beginning to feel sour, and not just in his stomach. With a glide, he was next to the sentinel. She didn't even turn her head. Her right hand was flat against the wall and the end of her left arm was hidden in the pocket of her black jacket. One of those coats for plus-sizes, dug up who knows where, that she always threw on her emaciated frame, which the slightest gust of wind could have blown over. No two ways about it, Albatrocious favored the scarecrow look. As if her stump wasn't already enough of a turn-off. No, she had to go one better, all the way to hermit-sustained-on-pride-sitting-on-a-fat-black-cloud, who forced you back to your vade retro and whose cousinhood with Gorgeous Gams had to be one of those weird laws of natural compensation. But, on this day of betrayal and defeat, the wounded general was of a mind to form an alliance with the doomsayer, who would make room for him on the black cloud and teach him how to call thunderbolts down upon those pathetic boobs who were trampling his *spolia opima* and angling for a slice of his cutie-pie. The latter writhed like a little sea serpent. With every jut of her hip, her skirt rode up and a wedge of naked flesh peeked between the scarlet banner and the black garter circling the top of her thigh. All this for that bunch of clods. And there she went, throwing her head back and showing off the rest, her bare throat and her nipples beneath the low-cut blouse. Anyone could get an eyeful just by peeking over. Enough to turn you off women for good, said the general, mortally wounded but still dignified, to the sentinel, whose existence, truth be told, had somewhat shattered his zoological classifications. He would unhesitatingly have listed her under indefinite entities, not pretty, not kittenish: encounters of a third kind, which comprised angels, invalids, nuns, witches, vegetarians, epileptics, and brainiacs, all of them completely nuts but none really dangerous. He even sometimes thought the sentinel (as it surely said in those books she was always lugging around in her pockets) was struggling against a *secret, and therefore all the more ardent, penchant* for her cousin's protector. And this, ipso facto, since day one. Barmy though she was, she must have felt passion coursing under her cracked skull the moment she caught sight of her general biting the dust over and over. Maybe there was still a way to turn the situation around. The beautiful loser routine was infallible. Back in the day, the pretty doll had shed more than one tear over it. Just a few more contorted grimaces and he'd have Nutcase in his pocket. Preferably the inner pocket. Instead of the wallet stuffed with IOUs. And snug against his frazzled heart, where he could murmur endearments to her, his face half buried in her raised collar, like a liaison officer slurring his mispronounced syllables into a hidden mike. He wasn't displeased with the little scenario he'd touched up for the occasion. It had been the perfect roadmap for luring in the pretty doll, back when her heartstrings could still be tugged and would vibrate whenever she asked herself the same questions she spent her time droning to strangers, plucked at random from the phonebook and from their torpor and blindsided with a wallop of anxiety that made them jerk like laboratory frogs: *about your life in general, would you consider yourself very satisfied, fairly satisfied, somewhat satisfied, or not at all satisfied?* At the other the other end of the line, panicked voices scraped the ditch of memory for some forgotten little pleasure that might miraculously still be lying around, calling out feebly; they tripped over a quavering intonation and rolled into the vast gutter, which drained its mud into the empty boxes where, hour after hour, the little fisherwomen planted their checkmarks. Even from this distance, the strangers plucked from the phonebook and from their torpor stank of mold. And the doll didn't want to end up like them, some survey statistic. She confided as much to her future protector, in the passageways between their little cubicles. He nodded his serious face, eyes ogling the gorgeous gams that clearly weren't made for rubbing against telephone cords ringing for losers who were only too glad to be pumped for their private information. Their feet were already growing roots. And along came this little sylph, shimmying like the telephone cord, to tickle their breadbasket, worry over whether their carcass ran on tap water or rotgut, stuffed itself with canned or frozen crapola. Or to learn if their precious third leg (which, off the record, hadn't taken on any riders in weeks, not even the licensed operator), if their precious third leg, as I was saying, when it nestled in the dark, preferred the contact of cotton or silk, white or striped. Sometimes, the little sylphs went so far as to jab their finger in their subjects' souls and ask, in the voice of a night nurse who's seen it all before, whether they had a hard time just getting by in life. *He* had a hard time, did the routed general, and how. Not only here, now, in the authentic Norman inn that had turned into a field of dishonor, leaving him disemboweled, his cock-and-bull out of the pen. He was already stitched from head to foot. With scars all up and down his back and, instead of medals, a string of raw red wounds over his heart. He was already heading for the ranks of old veterans. Without having won a single victory. Without even, truth be told, having waged a single battle. The eternal reservist, awaiting the engagement of the century—the next shot would be the one. The more things went on, the harder a time he had just getting by in life and the more content he was replaying the verbally incontinent tribune. But at his words, even the scars up and down his back yawned with boredom, and on his heart the wounds smirked knowingly. He had already tried that one out on them. After every good buzz, the pain returned. And to calm it, always the same expedients, the same menial jobs, the same scrapes of the same bottom of the same barrel, and, before month's end, the same raging fist shaken at the turnstiles that ate his smart cards and blinked their green eye in cold apology for having relieved the old clot of his last visible sign of wealth. The wallet swelled with a new crop of IOUs and squeezed, cuddly and faithful, against his breast, right where Baby used to lay her head, way back when. Back then, she pampered the statue of her protector. She stood on tiptoe and rested her head on the great man's chest. She strained her ear. Inside, the wallet was already just a debt incubator, but Baby still believed the wind was going to turn. While awaiting the great harvest, she tried to make herself small and slip into his inner pocket. She would wait there, perched on her gorgeous gams, elbows resting on the hem of the pocket as if on a balcony, and with little yelps of excitement would catch the banknotes as they came swirling in. But instead, the miniature pin-up had seen only IOUs, like a swarm of black moths in her clear sky. Disillusionment rained down. No more fairy tales. The pin-up had regained her wits, unfolded her legs, and jumped to earth to get away as fast as possible from the fantasy bubble in which she'd shut herself to counter the great protector's rantings. And so it was that at the authentic Norman inn, Theo the chastised started in again with Albatrocious, whom his cooings would surely end up enticing into the bubble, where the bird of ill omen would make an odd little one-handed pin-up, fastened to the wallet bursting with IOUs. If she would just turn her head his way, he'd teach her her role. But she looked like she was already in another movie. With the glazed stare of a psychotic gangster, her mitt blown off during a heist, her accomplices hurtling even then toward the authentic Norman inn to wipe out this bunch of losers who were clogging Theo's sight and hearing—Theo, who blew every fuse under his lid one by one and, firmly mired in his belligerence, projected a punitive exploit on his private movie screen, coating the walls of the inn in a scarlet bloodbath to avenge his lost honor.

Congealed duck's blood to follow the bird's nests: that's what my cousin had planned to cook up for her wedding. Duck's blood with basil, served chilled, just after the soup with its white lacework. Red clots on the diaphanous embroidery. Crude after refined. Royal fare to whet the appetite and, to spur it on, a taste of the bizarre. Congealed blood, flavored with basil and crushed roasted peanuts, in a large serving dish of fine porcelain. On the side, in a rectangular plate, slices of tender braised duck. Another of Grandmother's recipes, who toward the end could only breathe in the aroma of meat, bring a small piece to her mouth, suck out the juice, then put it back, intact, shining with a fine coat of saliva. The secret to congealed duck's blood was inscribed not in the codex but on a loose sheet, slipped between the back of the notebook and the plastified cover, among other witch's spells. Recipes my cousin had never prepared, but which she liked to refine, sitting in her empty house, in a tête-à-tête with the radio. The recipes consigned to the notebook had been dictated by Grandmother, some copied unaltered in their original tongue, others translated into French—the departed grandmother's voice was muffled either way. And each time my cousin opened her codex in the gleaming solitude, the ghost of Lady Jackal flew out to inspect the spanking new kitchen, sniff out the reek of burnt fat, lift the lids from the casseroles on the stove, lean over the yawning freezer, run her beady cop-from-hell eyes over the pantry, and cluck her tongue in disapproval, because everything smelled of cleanser and disinfectant, while the strange and subtle aromas enfolded in the codex had never settled on the film of boredom seeping down the walls. The jackal's spiteful howling burst from all over, jamming the radio waves and infiltrating the set, which crackled the phantom's grievances into my cousin's brain. Her ears were ringing from that sounding-off and, through the fissures of her crazed noggin, the chill wind of a guilty conscience filled her head, spread through her body, wrested her from her bulimic torpor. Even the gurgling in the sink imitated Grandmother's stifled sobs, who would die for real if she couldn't come to the gleaming kitchen to sniff the comforting aromas of the recipes in the codex. The ghost had already been betrayed on Wedding Day, left behind in the new house still empty of furniture, in the bare kitchen that smelled of paint and bleach. It yowled like a wounded jackal, dragging itself across the gleaming floor tiles, abandoned there by my cousin who was supposed to feed it on her wedding day with congealed duck's blood and bird's nests. But instead of turning the gleaming kitchen into an aromatic lararium, the ingrate had left Grandmother's sniffling ghost and gone off to live it up in an authentic Norman inn, where gold had flowed from every place setting and poured its warm larvae down every throat. The famished jackal lurking behind my cousin had been waiting lunations for these nuptials to quench its thirst with congealed duck's blood flavored with basil and to plunge its snout into the steaming effluvia of salangane algae. My cousin was supposed to open the secret codex and release the whole bouquet of forgotten smells, a royal tribute paid to the ghost so that it wouldn't come yelping around the gleaming house, where a spanking new life was growing in the shade of a wall of Germanic good sense, under a hood that sucked up odors, in a silence that smelled of disinfectant, behind the glass doors streaming with condensed boredom that concealed the shadows grimacing in the garden outside. But of congealed duck's blood there was none that wedding day. The bloodless phantom wandered in the empty house, where only a king-size bed had been delivered and installed in the bedroom. With plaintive little yips, Grandmother lay down at the foot of the bed, curled into a ball, and her vengeful spirit flew off to spoil the party in the authentic Norman inn, where it arrived just as the wedding cake was being set up amid the empty tables. The jackal's ghost prowled around the dark garden and bided its time, muzzle pressed against the windows of the inn; since the revelers were not returning to the lit room, it plunged into the abyss of perdition through an open skylight. It landed in the restroom of the authentic inn, under the heavy blast of a cannonade that made the walls shake. The boom-booms came from on high. The enemy was striking the ground to the beat and at full tilt. Grandmother frowned, clucking her tongue in disapproval. The little ingrates were dancing the java, their bellies saturated with gold; they couldn't care less about the hungry ghost, who had vindictive energy to burn and an infernal scheme to spoil the celebration. Crouching in a corner near the restrooms, Grandmother sent out waves of destructive energy, which spread through the authentic inn just as the revelers returned to the large ballroom, exclaiming their delight at the wedding cake. Grandmother's vengeful spirit swirled around and around that buttercream folly, threaded in and out between the black-clad legs, and spread its pernicious fluid like a shadow on the revelers, who felt a chill wind bite the backs of their necks, descend along their spines, and nest in the small of their backs. The chandeliers began to quiver above their heads. The buttercream folly swelled before their eyes like an inflated rubber bridegroom, about to explode under the revelers' noses and smack their faces white. The avenging spirit squatted on the buffet table, leapt from one loudspeaker to the other. The boom-booms sputtered out, leaving the joyous assembly petrified, mouths agape, their terrified kissers tossing this way and that. Their stomachs began to churn. Something grumbled in the abyss.

73

The flow of molten gold reversed course, or maybe the game animals were disgorging the rest of their blood. As the chandeliers spun faster and faster, the revelers' masks turned solid gray. The hullabaloo died down. The wedding cake swelled like Venus Gravida, dominating this carnival of shadows, this gala of the green. From the wings, where everything was going haywire—speakers blown, control knobs dead—a wilted emcee rushed in with a last gasp of enthusiasm and a final life raft for the drowning, whom he roused to a refreshing farandole. At his signal, the guests set in motion around the wedding cake. The emcee jollied himself hoarse, limply imitated by a raspy soloist. The little group circled with the gaiety of a coma, under the light of the chandeliers that began to tremble. The bulbs let out a muffled explosion and the authentic inn was plunged into darkness. The panicked revelers, frozen in place, gripped onto each other with a shudder. Without skipping a beat, the phantom saboteur leapt down from the chandelier and grabbed hold of the large rug covering the floor, on which the little group had just halted in mid-cavalcade. Grandmother yanked with all her deathly might and the rug slid, dragging with it the string of revelers teetering in the darkness. They tried to steady themselves on the wedding cake, only to send it flying with majestic abandon into the crowd, now strewn about the floor and smothered under a quilt of frosting. Grumbles of distress rose from the buttery muddle. The darkness was filled with cries and yelps. The black suits, now sporting cream dickeys, rose painfully, pushing away the knot of black-stockinged legs tangled in a twist of frosted lace. Candles appeared, throwing a compassionate light on the shipwrecked figures mucking about in the sea of pastry. The emcee, looking like a mummy wrapped in strips of chantilly, was the first to emerge from the disaster; by the light of the candles, he wiped away his creamy rind with a casual finger, licking it with a forced laugh, savoring the foamy spray vomited up by the Venus Gravida who, he said, must have been so eager to kiss him that she'd lost her footing. But the paunches around him were in no mood for levity and the legs were too busy pedaling forlornly in the frosting. The revelers sludged about in the white pastry rubble. They staggered, pale and silent under the charitable eye of the candles, like tin soldiers poorly repaired after being whupped by an unseen foe. What tornado had sent them all crashing to the floor? No use rubbing snow-flecked lids or peering into the darkness with fearful eyes: the vengeful spirit had already packed up her destructive outbursts and joyously bid farewell to the devastated guests. They stood there, downcast, chests and stomachs smeared, scratching their heads, biting their fingernails, each one replaying the scene from the applause over the wedding cake to the tumble on the rug. First they had felt a bit funny, a bite in the neck, cold sweat on the back. Then they were lifted from the nice cozy wedding and thrown into a whirl-wind of frosting, where the sugar figurines of the bride and groom, ejected from the top of the cake and united in their opprobrium, now rolled to the feet of Theo, who owed the little group more than they would ever know—after all, it was their ostracism that had spared him the frosting bath. He savored his revenge in his dark corner, neglected by the little candles and the Venus Gravi-da's outburst. With the gluttonous smile of a beachcomber watch-ing shipwreck victims lashed by the milky sea, Theo the close call advanced the toe of his loafer, barely soiled by the white snot, and lightly kicked the sugar wedding couple, who rolled arm in arm over the carpet to land against a spike heel that nearly decapitated the groom. This journey was starting to look dangerous. The wed-ding couple, joined for better or worse, lay on their stomachs and buried their heads in the frosting pillow, showing everybody their chipped train and chocolate coattails, their joint despair drowned in the white carpet. The revelers, picking themselves up as best they could, formed a circle around the floating couple with its backsides in the air. They cast sad looks upon the poor little sugar creatures ejected from their pedestal, but no one bent over to fish them out. Heads lowered, faces pitiful, a wee bit nauseated and eager to finish with this blow-out cum meltdown, they all stood around the bodies like hired mourners who had run out of tears, wishing they could sneak off under cover of darkness, neither seen nor heard, and escape this nice cozy wedding that had been ravaged by a humorless ghost who was surely guarding the exits of the authentic inn, ready to give the first runaway a good hiding. The candles shed their wax tears at the desolate spectacle. It felt like a death vigil. A fly passed, then an angel. There was a cleared throat, a faint sigh, the sound of a heel tapping the damp carpet, but no one said a word. The avenging spirit had stolen everyone's tongue along with the lights. And the revelers stood there like wilted licorice wands, around the marzipan couple that had nose-dived into the cream to escape the phantom's strafing run. But Grandmother had already summoned back her avenging spirit, which swept through the restrooms and exited the authentic inn through the skylight and went to unleash the rest of its destructive energy in the spanking new house.

The recipe books were strewn about the gleaming floor, around the chair formerly occupied by my cousin, who had put down her codex to retire to the privy, commanding her sister as she went to pick up the culinary mess that clashed with the order and sparkle of the pantry. One butt cheek resting on the edge of the sink, bare feet skimming the ground, hand on her chin, my younger cousin languidly emerged from her meditative pose. She unglued her posterior from the sink, leaving on the stainless steel the aureole of a kiss. With the edge of her bare foot, she herded together the dispersed volumes and, leaning forward, stacked them up while emitting sighs of eternal boredom. She lugged the pile to the gleaming counter, opened one of the upper cabinets, shoved the whole thing inside, and slammed the door. She had kept with her the secret codex, which she began to peruse in turn, chewing on her thumb. The round ants of blue ink ran over the paper, buzzing in a strange language that blended Grandmother's sour intonations with the voice of King Lear, which occasionally seeped through a chink in her memory as if from the prompter's pit and tossed center stage a few syllables of the idiom dragged out of storage: an incomprehensible word decorated with a half-moon crown, or three very short words with accents sticking out in all directions. It tinkled like bells on the collar of a lost dog. At night, it made a devil of a racket. Worse than pots tied to a dog's tail. Most often, it was a continual murmur, a ghostly babble, which raised a dust cloud of unlearned words bristling with whimsical marks. All that verbal dust blew into the ears that were cute enough to nibble, but nostalgia could also be scraped out, and of the ghostly babble there remained only a bit of wax at the tip of a pinky finger. No sooner was all that word-dust cleared away than it was time to eliminate the long-lost aromas. Cooking aromas that wafted back to tickle the nostrils. Smells of steaming yams sliced lengthwise and dusted with sugar. Of green fruits sprinkled with salt and red pepper. Of words whispered at naptime. The scent of the abjured idiom returning to titillate the buds of memory. But my cousin's memory was well ventilated. The moment the smoke of nostalgia stung her eyes, a vent opened, airing out the acrid odors. Then all one could smell around the nymph was the perfume of a young girl, skin polished, fur brushed smooth, pores exuding a scent of emotional asepsis devoid of nostalgic microbes. My sweet-smelling cousin sat down on the floor, back against the wall. The curves of her long legs reflected in the gleaming tiles, she leaned toward the codex that she held upright, resting it on the row of metal buttons on her cutoffs, the fringes brushing over her thighs like a curtain of eyelashes over a brazen stare. She intoned one of Grandmother's recipes. Lips pouting, a finger caressing each word, she readied herself to pursue the unfamiliar column of blue ants. She stalled against a funny accent shaped like an upside-down caduceus, tried out different inflections like a burglar jingling his ring of keys at a recalcitrant lock, got nowhere, gurgled, sputtered, started from scratch, licked her lips, brushed away a lock of hair, put on a serious face, cleared her throat, quickened her delivery, scattered a few diacriticals along her stations of the cross, emitted a few cries of exasperation, and finally threw in the towel, tossing away the codex that came to rest under the table. My cousin bent forward, touching her fingers to her toes. She remained in that position, hair cascading down, eyes squinting toward the abecedary of her origins. Anyway, she never had learned to decipher those hieroglyphic ants. When she bothered, she managed laboriously to sound out bits and pieces of King Lear's gibberish, but it was too much work for ramblings that didn't even ramble, since King Lear was of the I'd-rather-die-than-open-my-heart school. Still, it was better than having to hear them read aloud by their titular addressee, who, the minute a letter was received, hopped on the phone, called Rue Glacière or the telemarketing firm, and delivered her recitation, with simultaneous translation and, as a bonus, the sour pinched voice of Grandmother, exhumed for the occasion. My cousin sat back up, stretched lazily, and went to fetch the codex, which was indifferently displaying its white, ant-speckled belly. She poked her nose into the blue anthill and sniffed one last grandmotherly recipe, scratching her head at the mystery of the *o*'s and *u*'s embellished with a little trinket stuck on its temple ơ and sometimes crowned with a sign hanging in the air, like an upright hook ǒ. A whole cockeyed hardware, dancing before the eyes of the would-be sleuth who puffed her cheeks with impatience at the droning enigma. The enigma listed the ingredients for duck's blood flavored with basil and crushed peanuts. Behind the tinkling of the cockeyed hardware rattled Grandmother's voice, recommending that the slices of braised duck be served on the side, that finely chopped basil be spread evenly over the congealed duck's blood, and that three especially fragrant leaves be set aside as garnish. My cousin stifled a yawn, biting the tip of her thumb. The air in the kitchen, cleansed by the range hood that had been humming since consumption of the squid Provençal, filled with the effluvia of dominical indolence. My cousin shut the codex. She wouldn't have minded seeing flavored duck's blood at the famous feast. What a face the groom's sixty-six guests would have pulled! Vampire fare at the union of virtue and temperance! So instead, everyone had been put on a Germanic regimen and gorged on deer's blood. The banquet was pretty memorable all the same. Little Sister had liked it. Next to the groom's sixty-six guests, who feasted while talking nutsandbolts, the bridal party did not make a very presentable escort. There was Southpaw bringing up the rear, big-mouth Theo who always opened it when he shouldn't, Little Sister's gorgeous gams, not sorry to be offered a whole retinue of new admirers, and Grandmother's ghost, which had invited itself to dessert and treated the celebrants to a terror supreme and a cream whipping. And Southpaw hadn't even made one of her dire predictions that time! She had even given a little thought to her getup for once. Her black jacket, cut to fit three of her, was rumpled, but with a touch of class. During the meal, she had kept very quiet, her stump buried in her pocket. She sat almost opposite Theo at the end of the table, next to a vociferous three-piece suit busily stuffing his dandified gullet and murmuring sweet nothings to a pale pink ensemble with raised collar, who, once irrigated with Graves, opened like a morning glory, cooed full-throatedly, and jabbed her elbow into the neighboring breadbasket, which looked to be suffocating beneath the row of buttons lining the pearl-gray vest that matched its razor-sharp suit. Southpaw had let the flow of warm gold coagulate without swallowing a single nugget. The slices of deer shed the rest of their blood into the dish, which she had pushed away with a grimace. She had loosened her lips only to absorb some Graves. But instead of growing flushed, her mask turned celadon green. She had always been a finicky eater, even before her paw went south. She picked, nibbled, made a face. Eats turned her stomach, drink made her gag. She folded her arms and, with the eyes of an executioner who knew a thing or two about the condemned man's last wish, watched the others gobble down the swill. She had a way of making you feel like a pig, snout in the trough, spine pierced by the rain of lances that her glacial abstemiousness called down from above. But it all tasted so good. They ignored the abstainer, who wasn't going to spoil it for them, those crab fritters plunged into thick, spicy sauce, leaving on the fingers greasy little pearls licked off with an indecent satiety that burned your lips and made your ears red. Southpaw spat on all the dishes prepared from Grandmother's recipes. The crab fritters, the pig's ears in vinaigrette—she had never touched a one. Nothing but poison, she said. Jackal poison. And at the table she held her breath, to keep from being contaminated. She didn't appreciate the Germanic fare, either. Just barely did Miss I'll-have-none-of-that deign to grant it a gram of polite attention. And whatever you do, don't suggest she just try a taste. You could plop a hunk of deadwood in her plate—same diff. At the wedding, she had watched the concoctions parade by, letting the molten gold congeal, the deer's blood freeze. She sat stiff as a rail, left arm under the table, right hand lying next to her dish. She trained her hangman's look on her left-hand neighbor, the wearer of the razor-sharp suit, who swallowed quickly, chewed heavily, made every mouthful go down with gurgles of satisfaction. Southpaw stared at the gobbler's neck while stroking the handle of her knife, which had not been dipped in deer's blood. Around her plate, the tablecloth remained immaculate. Next to her, the white square occupied by the wrinkler of the razor-sharp suit was speckled with brownish stains overlaid by the flying spittle that Theo the unclean spattered onto the table from across the way, drowning in Graves the promises made the night before on the futon pillow, cross his heart and hope to die, that he would behave like a grand duke on a state visit, wouldn't open his yap, wouldn't brag his head off, wouldn't lift an elbow, wouldn't neglect his other half of the sky, and would keep his nervous laughter in check, since it always made people uneasy. He had reiterated his Decalogue over and over, before nodding off. But after a few unauthorized glasses, the commandments flew out the window. Now there was no stopping the conspirator, who again imagined himself captain of this ship, free to launch into his ranting raves (as Southpaw would say) and to trample the terms of the partnership agreement hammered out after a quick survey on the drawbacks of shacking up (another of the witch's darts). *Do you find living together thrilling (in the short term)? trying (in the long term)? absurd (from start to finish)? ego-crushing (daily)? demoralizing (night after night)? an experience of brief mutual communion followed by long reciprocal humiliation (or, how can you reach orgasm when desire is dead)? of deceitful incomprehension mutated into blatant indifference (or, the pleasure of giving up solving a puzzle when you've gained nothing from it)? the memory of territories conceded with quavering voices and repossessed without warning, nose thumbed as an added flourish (or, the pleasure of finally feeling nice and comfy after spending years on the procrustean bed)?* No way, then, to shut off her infernal half, who was barking like an untethered Cerberus. The booted kicks under the table had only spurred the animal on. But the crowning touch was when he'd gone over to stand on his hind legs and press up against Southpaw. While everyone was dancing the samba, to sweat out a little doe's blood, Theo the forsaken had gone to sniff around the cousin who'd never been close to his fickle heart and whom he referred to as either Lethal Potion or Albatrocious. He never passed up a chance to mock her cousin. He stuffed books into his pockets and mimicked her walk, hunched over, stoop-shouldered, like an old crone with vigilante eyes. He shoved his left hand into his jacket and imitated the dark voice she used when, out of the blue, at the table, she began muttering *He's not crazy!* Around her, they pretended not to hear. For years she'd been blurting, just like that, in the middle of a meal, her little phrase that brought everybody down. She always chose the perfect moment to puff into her blowgun. The poisoned dart landed smack in the heart of the tasty little Sunday dish. The toxic vapors spread, just as the diners' mouths were beginning to water, their nostrils to dilate, their tongues to hang out. Everyone fell silent, kneading a piece of bread, caressing the stem of their wineglass up, down, and back up, pulling on their skirt, looking fixedly at their nails, like a rodent going through withdrawal, or rumpling a corner of their napkin, eyes glued to the hem, hypnotized, deaf, and mute all at once. The malaise lasted only two or three leaden minutes, until someone shook himself and roused the others. At which point the chatting got back on track, joyously accompanied by the clinking of forks. And Southpaw could keep on grumbling *He's not crazy! He's not crazy!*—all around her they scraped the bottom of the good little dish, wiped their mouths, regretting that it was already finished and plying each other with idiocies so as not to hear the bird of ill omen. But the odd thing was, sitting like that before her empty plate and croaking *He'snotcrazy,* she didn't look like the bird of ill omen that she was on other days. Her sad tomato face took on a bit of color, as if lit by a small candle from within. And her eyes, for once, didn't remind you of two swamps with corpses at the bottom. *He'snotcrazy! He'snotcrazy!* Theo repeated the incantation in the voice of a sinister blackbird. To add to the impression, he even made his face look like Albatrocious, hair flat and parted in the middle, cheeks sunken. And after all that, he goes to rub up against the bird of ill omen the moment he felt cast off by the wedding guests. Whatever could he have whispered to her? She hadn't even turned her head when he'd walked up, moistening his lips and running his palm over his little blond forelock. He had stayed there a good while, back to the wall, almost glued to Southpaw, chatting her up while puffing on his cigarette, which he pinched between thumb and forefinger to look tough. He'd always claimed that her cousin, with her aura of a chipped icon, probably went for hoods, tough guys, small-timers, and the like. What could he have murmured into her ear, while the twist and the samba were finally putting some ambiance into the celebration that had been snoozing big time?

The gentleman was trying to gain a foothold. But Southpaw didn't seem exactly bowled over by the boarding attempt. She had looked away, toward the door, as if waiting for her chance to slip out. And poor Theo kept rowing, rowing, rowing, without ever reaching Dead Man's Island. The more he played at Mr. Suave, the more Albatrocious pulled into her great black shell. Her sad tomato exhaled its last bit of color. Nothing left on her palette but a cadaverous green. But the corpse still had some kick left in her. Abruptly ditching Theo the bird-catcher—who stood there flabbergasted, bird-call between his teeth—she had beaten a path to the restrooms, cheeks bloodless, hand over her mouth, ready to spew up the milk and honey poured into her ear. She had hidden out for a good while. To puke up the wedding, vomit out the others' binge. Her sad tomato face had finally resurfaced even so, concealed behind the château of butter frosting. Immediately after, everything had gone haywire. The light bulbs had fainted, the tunes choked. The carpet had sprouted wings. And before they'd realized it they were standing on a carpet that had aspirations of flying, and the revelers had found themselves with all four hooves in the air. With a whinny of distress, they were buried under the cream rubble of the château, which had collapsed at this breach of decorum. From the back of the room, Southpaw watched the spectacle. A strange smile blazed in the middle of her sad tomato.

The wedding photos had arrived in a large envelope, dropped by one of those airborne lice that furrowed the blue vellum above Saigon. King Lear was watering his garden, under the watchful eye of the Wheezer, who had been kept in bed all week by a bout of malaria and had arrived at the gate of the blue house early that morning for his little pick-me-up, craving those lousy eels that had appeared to him in slimy parades, mocking him for seven feverish days and nights. They stretched out before him, long, dark, roly-poly, and slippery. Enough to drive a sleeper who was already going stir-crazy off the deep end. Barely recovered, his body still shaking, the Wheezer had slammed his door behind him and hoofed it to his friend's: he needed a good double portion to put him right. So imagine his sentiments toward the large envelope that, no doubt about it, would scramble King Lear's brains, make his hands shake and his eyes tear up. And the eels would be ruined. There was no room in cooking for emotion. You needed a steady hand, a clear eye, a precise chop, an expert slice. At the first sight of the large envelope, the bugger had already spilled half his water and trod on a clump of perky little flowers, which had bedded out during the Wheezer's eclipse. In the time it took to bring the envelope inside, King Lear had mastered his pounding ticker. He righted the trampled flowers and the two friends went off together to market. The envelope remained on the table. When they returned, the Wheezer saw that it hadn't been opened. He turned it over several times, gauged its weight. Obviously it was the little ones showing off again, a full bundle in color. King Lear would spend another night making collages, pasting the gloss-paper wings of his escaped butterflies into his album, and the next day he wouldn't exactly be tip-top; he'd be wearing his sullen face, would hit the wall with his fist, toss pots and pans on the floor, flick off the heads of flowers that hadn't had their baptism, neglect the eels—the Wheezer would get only a little dry sausage to munch on, until the fit subsided or the fidget-ass headed to the seashore, from where he'd return with his head on straight and a plump eel in his shopping bag. This time, the anticipated catastrophe was a bit longer in coming. Depending on that day's rituals, the large pastel envelope with its navy hiblue border was moved from table to bed, bed to table, but its contents remained sealed. The more time went by, the more the envelope swelled with mystery. As if it were a small square cut from the blue vellum itself and thrown into King Lear's little corner, like a delicacy bestowed by the Great Deaf-Mute. He always let a few crumbs fall, to make it look as if mercy were dogging His heels. The Wheezer recognized Him perfectly in this way of tossing His disconsolate pups a bone now and again, except that the marrow was laced with slow-acting poison. At first King Lear circled around the bone with suspicious growls; then he started to yip in excitement. He had a whole catalogue of the little ones' preening. A complete collection that he fanned out among his flowers, sitting on his doorstep in the evening, just before night fell hard like a curtain on the princesses' simpering, their coy little winks, cute little pouts, and charming giggles, which King Lear caressed softly so as not to scratch their soft skin with his calloused hands. The Wheezer was offered an eyeful. He ogled the little ones' affectations with copious nods, pretending to be delighted by all this to-do, but it was just to stay on good terms with King Lear, who devoured his princesses with famished eyes. The Wheezer made the same eyes when he caught the scent of grilled eels. Moreover, all he had to do to fool his friend was picture, instead of the little ones and their flounces, a sea serpent in its brown robe, captured in mid-undulation and thoroughly examined before being dispatched by the cleaver. While King Lear turned the pages, the Wheezer pursued his raspy commentary. For years he had played at being wonderstruck. The little ones got bigger, their preening grew more refined, their attractions lovelier to behold. One wearing silk blouses, her hair in a distinguished bun; the other more brazen, with skirts that showed off her pins well above the knee. King Lear shoved them both under the Wheezer's nose. They gave off a scent of clean hair, sweetened skin, pink nails, pulpy lips. Especially the young one, who didn't seem cold around the eyes or legs, a cute little eel freshly skinned and rubbed in salt, just waiting to get done. The older one, beneath her furbelows, was dowdier. A heavy, slow-moving, but robust eel that you'd have to grip tightly with both hands. She'd ended up getting caught nevertheless. In the pastel envelope with its navy border, she must have looked entirely different, circling in those nuptial waters. And her angler, the one who'd managed to grab hold of the dowdy eel, what sort of mug did he have? The Wheezer had heard the besotted one had a thing for spirituality. When King Lear poured out the contents of the pastel envelope, he'd have to anticipate a meditative head popping up between the two simpering princesses. But the envelope remained sealed and the Wheezer, who'd pulled a sour face when he saw it plunk down among the flowers, now started to chomp at the bit. All that mystery was spoiling the taste of his eels. The secrecy was weighing on his stomach. Circle as he might around the envelope, fingering it, gauging its weight, sniffing at it like a weasel, the other remained impassive. Then one morning, arriving at the blue house, he found King Lear decked in his swanky suit just fished out of the closet. The envelope was open and the little ones' hijinks spread over the table. No getting around it, the princesses really caught your eye with their perky flounces and their smiles freshly painted for the occasion. The besotted-one-with-a-thing-for-spirituality had the zealous face of an eel who'd chop himself in slices for his better half. On top of which, he had rosy cheeks, blue eyes, a pointed beard, and was built like a house. Hearty stuff, at first blush; rock solid. Not a chink or a crack. In his custom-fit suit cut by the best snip in Saigon, King Lear was enacting a repeat performance of the wedding with the photos arranged in ceremonial order, in longer and longer rows that fanned out over the table. The Wheezer circled around it all and, in his sepulchral voice, coughed up his most apt commentary, just to stroke the fur of that paternal old beast, moved by the favor the Great Deaf-Mute had granted from on high, so perfectly making the bed in which the princess of the distinguished chignon lay. King Lear feasted on the wedding leftovers. He smiled gratefully at the Great Bestower, who had placed the plump eel in the hands of such an industrious angler. The Wheezer circled around the table, pronounced his raspy benediction. Now they just had to pluck the younger one: may the Great Bestower toss a nice bird-catcher into her slender claws, and then the old stock of the family tree could peacefully let himself rot in his blue house. For some time already the old stock had felt his roots withering away. His trunk creaked with every effort, and with every effort a bit more of the old stock crumbled into earth and returned to dust. King Lear was making his bed, the pit where he'd soon go to his final rest. He had bought a small rectangular plot in a country graveyard, near a pond. The sun beat down on the graves, but the groundskeeper had received authorization to plant some trees. Old Lear would decompose in the shade, in royal tranquility, rocked by the rustle of bamboo and the lapping of wavelets. If he felt like splurging, his bed could also be ringed with flowers that would be watered every day, flowers he'd nourish with his carcass. They grew quickly around here. Before choosing his pit, King Lear had had a good look around the place. Large, voracious excrescences lay over the graves, invading the stones and devouring the inscriptions. The groundskeeper couldn't keep up with it all. And yet, this corner of the cemetery had only emaciated old folks, who had kicked it before the saprophytes returned to fatten Saigon up again. All they had was their dry skin and bones about to crumble to dust. Bones that shuddered with the memory of scrambles in the night, under the rain, before the state-run shops where, as compensation, a barker dispensed a fistful of moldy rice. These were skeletons that someone had simply thrown in the ground. Bags of bones that had lived on rotting, stringy, worm-eaten scraps. They were light, so, so light, in their coffins, tossed into their holes like kindling. But seeing the beautiful flowers sprouting from their detritus, you might believe they had some reserves of strength after all. Those starving, indoctrinated oldsters, pulled this way and that, were the kind of fertilizer you couldn't get anymore. Twelve feet under and they were still hard at work. Young people today would do well to take a page from their book: so the groundskeeper said to anyone who'd listen. He saw them ride up, their faces all pink, fresh, and greasy. They came on their putt-putts. The few steps from their machines to the tomb left them sweating like sick hogs. Three little bows, two

sticks of incense in front of the ancestor's cameo, and pffft! Off
they went, straddling their rocket ships. When that bunch went
into the ground, don't expect them to fertilize the flowers! They'd
keep everything for themselves: their rolls of fat, stocky bones,
thick hair, and gold teeth, just like the rich folk on the other side
of the graveyard who held it all in. The flowers on their tombs
were scraggly; though watered day and night, they looked like de-
formed fetuses. Old Lear would be like a king on his throne over
there by the pond, counting the stars in the night sky. In the morning, birds would come to peck near the water. At dusk the flowers would blanket him, while crickets played their sonatina. It
sounds so good you almost want to go lie down in it right now,
the Wheezer had said, savoring the humor, but not the idea of his
cook departing this life. He himself clung at all costs to the here-
below, certain that up there with the Great Deaf-Mute they also
dined every day, but not on grilled eel. In his cavernous voice, he
blessed the rectangular plot of earth King Lear had bought, heart
aflutter in hopes of one day seeing his little ones there, heads veiled
in white, heads lowered, hands folded, having rushed in from the
other hemisphere to weep over the old man in his pit. The Wheezer
made it his business to keep the old man from going there quite
yet, cheer him up in every way possible, sure that the bugger just
needed to shake up his sad sack. But trying to put a smile on that
wretched prune was like tickling a skinned, desiccated eel. The
Wheezer could barely squeeze a grimace out of him by miming
operatic arias — the climactic scene when the virgin poses as a
bonze and, tears, sighs, faintness, face hidden behind the ample
sleeve, sends away her lover who has come ringing *ding dong!* at
the door of her monastery. He put a lot of himself into those an-
tics, hoping to make King Lear split his sides. But whenever he
managed to pour some balm on his wounds, the skinned old coot
opened them again and doused them with salt. Still more of the
Great Deaf-Mute's mischief. He enjoyed seeing all those wounds,
those open faces straining toward Him, though He heard noth-

ing and stared in amazement at all those chicks with their gaping beaks, who could cheep and cheep, but the blue screen blocked their plaintive warbling. When the Great Deaf-Mute peeked through the vellum, He saw only long, spindly necks; mouths yawning but silent. And, depending on His mood, He either dropped a slug into an open beak or dispatched a predator to wipe out the whole supplicant brood. King Lear sat there, mouth and wounds wide open, waiting for the next punishment. The paternal old beast wanted to deflect the hand of the Great Peon, so that He might spare the princesses, who were asking for trouble. The tanned old hide was offering itself as a whipping post to His bad mood. It could make you laugh until you cried, the Wheezer thought. The more he taunted the Great Peon, the more King Lear turned catechumenal. The Wheezer didn't know whether to attribute it to fatherly sentimentality or to heebie-jeebies over his impending demise. As long as King Lear's expert hand gripped, struck, and skinned the eels destined for the grill, the Wheezer could rest easy—for however many months he had left. Because he knew that, even if he hung on as hard as he could (and he certainly didn't intend to raise anchor before having his fill of sea serpents), even if he clung to the docks like a lunatic, he couldn't push his winded mechanism, rusted parts, and sibilant rattle much farther. All things considered, he was perfectly happy that they'd pulled him out of his damp pit and granted him a reprieve, reasonably well spent as King Lear's jester, eel taster, and carnival martyr. With his routine, the torture victim released from his pillory, he had soaked the faithful to finance his unexpected extension. Now that his debt was paid up—the Great Deaf-Mute had his spot-clean pad, filled morning till night with lambs come to bleat their hymn of thanksgiving—the Wheezer felt his spool unwinding with insidious haste. The main thing was to reach the end before King Lear went to lie down in his hole, with his stars, crickets, and bamboo, leaving the kitchen empty, the fire out, the eels pardoned, and his tablemate famished. The Wheezer was on the watch. The bone he was picking with the Great Deaf-Mute threatened to jab him in the rear and spirit away King Lear first. And the jester would be left there all alone, deprived of his little pleasures. Oh, but he had a fallback plan! He'd march right off and throw himself into an eel hatchery. No gravesite. No frills. Just a cortege of nice plump serpents to do the honors.

Do you think about death? Very often (the death of others, everyone who ever left you in a jam: if only they would clear out, croak with their mouths wide open)—seldom (no use wasting time getting bogged down with thoughts about the omega)—never (it's bad for the *complexion). Do you believe in another life? Yes (if second chance)—no (if you have to pay for your sins)—no opinion (you call this a life?). Would you like to be reincarnated as an old spider whose only concern is weaving its web? Yes (to scare girls with!)— no (ewww! ewww!)—don't know (can a water spider, once on land, turn into a sylph?). Would you like to communicate with the dead? Yes (to slack off at work)—no (what language do ghosts speak, any- way?)—don't know (earth zombies are already a handful, so spir- its . . .).* Pinky extended and raised thumb glued to her left ear, my younger cousin improvised a metaphysical telephone survey. She did both questions and answers, varying her delivery. A hesitant frown, a knit of the brow, a flare of the nostrils, a sigh of impa- tience, a prim fluty voice, tracks of teeth biting her lower lip, the whole thing punctuated by some exclamations dropping like pearls from a snatched necklace. Arranged before her, on a large white plate, lay wafer-thin slices of raw ham that she separated with the tips of her fingers. She swallowed them slowly, head tilted back, between a mimic, a throaty laugh, and two impromptu answers to the ersatz survey. This prosciutto is delicious. Like lace. And the taste of it on your tongue! The fridge in the gleaming kitchen concealed some real treasures. Always something to set your taste buds dancing. It was by far the only consolation for these stran- glehold Sunday gatherings in the spanking new house. Beginning with memorable surprises at lunch. Exotic delicacies, unexpected sauces, unusual mixtures, delectable aromas. Enough to make a Stylite climb down from his column. And that was just the preamble. Afterward, at the first yawn of boredom, you only had to stick your nose in the fridge and help yourself to the leftovers, like a tomb raider. *Do you believe in ghosts coming back to drag you away by the ankles? (The dead seize the quick, said Southpaw.) In the nine circles of Hell? (This wood, so harsh, dismal, and wild, uttered the sphinx, standing by the stove.) In the wandering of souls who can't find rest? (Men were we, and are now turned each to a tree, the cousin piped up again, trying to be interesting.)* Another slice of *prosciutto crudo.* The last one. There was still some cured beef in the fridge. And a full jar of gherkins. Plunge one's fingers into the brine, pluck out one of those slender, crunchy little pickles. Savor them as they are, one by one, jar in hand. (*And what about the death of King Lear? said Southpaw.*) Better still, enjoy those tasty morsels with a dab of strong mustard. It stung, tickled your belly. Not bad at all. As a last little treat, a few crunchy flutes, with a drop of wine left over from lunch. (*What about the old man's death, do you think about that? Very often, seldom, never? Southpaw in her corner was talking to no one but herself.*) Still, have to watch the waistline. Tonight, there were lamb's brains on the menu. Not very exciting, compared with thick grilled steaks last time. But the Lamaist wanted to eat plain and dreary, just some brains and light vegetables, to avoid waking up in the middle of the night feeling around for his digestion pills. He was kind of a joke, that brother-in-law of hers, with his fanatical meditations. Spiritual elevation on Sundays after the feast, rumbling dyspepsia and draconian layaway plans the rest of the week. Still, a good enough egg. A meditative Atlas always ready to take on your burden along with his own. A scoutmaster, with his old bachelor ways, his penny-pinching economies, his droning voice, his morose sentences, and the occasional limp wisecrack ruminated all through dinner and finally spat out at dessert, to the delight of the impish wag himself who followed it with a guffaw, undeterred by the silence around the table and the consternated little grimace on everyone's face. (*And King Lear's burial, do you think about that? Very often, seldom, never? the amputee muttered, pacing around the kitchen.*) Once he had shot his naughty bolt and barked his broad laugh, the meditator retreated back into his shell, absorbed once more in his spiritual pains or savings plans, serious as a turtle nibbling at his lettuce leaf; scout's honor, he would say nothing spicy or saucy for the rest of the day. Not another word. Not another covert glance at Little Sister's bare legs, twisting around each other to combat the boredom—and still the hands on the mantelpiece clock turned no faster and Sunday dragged on, heavy as the head of a catoblepas. The meditator, with his leaden skull and long, flaccid neck, looked something like a melancholic catoblepas with a pointy beard. Sometimes on Sundays he remained in his corner, head drooping, eyes glued to his plate or his feet. He didn't look at anyone, didn't have any keen gadgets to show off or doodads to display. He didn't even shoot off his fiery wisecrack during the meal. When he was like that, with his weighty head hanging at the end of his long neck as if it were straining to roll across the floor, you had to brace yourself for a flood of adventures, later that evening, just before beddy-bye. The fabulous tale of his fabulous conversion, told until you couldn't stand it anymore, a tale everyone knew to the point of nausea. How one evening he took the boat for Elba Island. How the storm broke out. How the catoblepas, deathly ill, clung to a guardrail on the bridge. How an odd customer, with pointy beard and voluminous skull, spindly neck and solid gut, had come up to him and, as he was vomiting overboard his weary, lawless, faithless loner's soul, the odd customer "showed him the way," which was to the East, beneath the roof of the world. Good lord, but of course, the not-yet-meditator had said to himself, yakking all the harder. And when finally, exhausted by the reverse enema and the whipping rain, he let himself drop onto a bench, still maintaining a firm grip on the guardrail, the odd customer shouted into his open ear and mouth the ABC's of wisdom, *maya, tantra, tantaratara.* He decided to give it a whirl, just as the boat, after copious sarabands, washed up on Elba's shores. But this was not the end of the fabulous tale of his fabulous conversion, oh no. Heaven help the rash individual who rushed in to stem the tide or beg for mercy. Because then the catoblepas abruptly raised his weighty head and stared everyone in the eye. And that was the death sentence: every time you broke his momentum, he started over from the beginning, spinning it out even longer. How, one summer's evening, the boat navigating comfortably between Marseille and Elba. How the storm. How the elements. How deathly ill. How the ocean, the shroud. How a shouting messenger. How the blah-blah of wisdom. How all ears. How Maya tantra tantaratara. (*And what about King Lear's shroud, do you ever think of that? Very often, seldom, never? Southpaw's nose was plunged in her book; she fired off these macabre darts as if reading aloud.*) The meditator, in fact, worried about King Lear. He gladly imagined himself a converter, taking the hand of the lost old man, who'd been bamboozled by the sky pilots, the missionary snake-oil bastards, the church mice—the whole brotherhood of Bible-thumpers exported in the heyday of colonial trade to send the Terrors of Hell shivering down the natives' bent spines and sprinkle over their obtuse heads the stagnant water of holy civilization, the twice millennial *cloaca maxima.* Dixit the meditator. Now and then he lapsed into flights of lyrical protest, at which point he turned scarlet, banged his fist against the wall, the table, the armrest, and everyone gaped at him, flabbergasted to see red cannonballs spewing from a mouth normally so placid. (*And what about the old man's last rites, do you think of those? Southpaw pulled the pin on another grenade.*) When the meditator tore off his muzzle, he could be a real pit bull. He bared his fangs, howled for the kill, went for the jugular of the soul-befuddlers, the catechism-mumblers, collection plate–lickers, vinegar-guzzlers, the scramblers of young minds and fondlers of novices, exposing them all. The worst were the blackcoats with their gospels according to Saint Whatshisface, who'd gone to the colonies to inflict an earful on the miscreants. That's when they really opened the sluice gates on the twice millennial *cloaca maxima.* The lousy church mice, the turnkeys of the *cloaca maxima,* sent ripe cheese for their crusaders and used Bibles for the little pagans, which arrived in the tropical heat with a swarming halo of bluebottles. And still the gospel according to Saint Whatshisface spread the Good Word, teaching the little pagans that everything was their fault, their fault, their very grievous fault (strike! strike this sinner's heart!), but that by starving half to death they would soon enter the eye of the needle. The meditator, in full-fledged dyspeptic trial (so said Southpaw, who brooked no rivals when it came to grandiloquence, or a low mass), made mincemeat of priests at the Sunday table, raving like a lunatic. Just let me at those pulpiteers with their ratlike faces, one eye leering at celestial Jerusalem, the other sneering at sublimities—so long as the cheese is still good. Just give me one good shot at the huffing carrion spreading its contrite sweat, pious muck, and all the fine odors of civilization among the pagans (so they'll slave all the harder for those miserable plantation owners, once the first, soon the last—*they're* the ones who should change into camels to go through the eye of a needle). A real gang of celestial poisoners, who took themselves for miracle workers with their cure-all hoaxes, *Suffer and thou shalt have thy gratuity.* Lower your head, let yourself be shorn, good little lamb, and one day the Old Gypaetus will swoop down from the sky, squeeze you in his claws, and carry you off to his lair, where, as a reward for your bellyaching, *I am troubled, I am bowed down greatly, forsake me not, O Lord, O my God, be not far from me, make haste to help me, O Lord my salvation,* the Old Gypaetus will make haste to dig his long hooked beak into your heart just as it is bursting with hope, like the shipwrecked man who thought he'd reached the Halcyon. The meditator was sure he could yank the blinders off King

94

Lear, extract him from the needle's eye through which the old man labored to squeeze, if not his mishmash of broken bones, then at least his skull, obnubilated since the celestial rays had beaten down on it. Just let the agnus dei enter the spanking new house, and in two shakes of a lamb's peroration the meditator would turn him inside-out like a glove—assuming he could get his point across. But what language would he use to teach the ABC's of wisdom, since his better half had flatly refused to lend a hand? She already had to slave like a longshoreman just to hail the royal shipwreck and tug him to port, where the parapets still needed a good scrub-down—once the old hull was docked, no way was she about to go rummaging around its hold to mess with the cargo. It would just be a quick little stopover, enough time for King Lear to rinse his tub in waters softer than the skin of his off-spring, and then she made clear the wreck would head out again. Just so long as King Lear had a good time on his shore leave. After that, he'd have all eternity to deal with his soul and decide if he was bequeathing it to the Catechists, the Brahmans, the Sufis, or any other brand of charlatan. That shut the meditator's trap good and proper, shooing him back to his mantras. But good egg he was and good egg he remained; he immediately lowered his flag before the impending storm, if only to quiet his stomach, which already churned enough. Since that's how things stood, he'd keep for himself the ABC's of wisdom and go back to his corner to play the catoblepas, neck flaccid, head drooping, eyes lowered, lip zipped. Not a single gherkin left. Oops, she'd emptied the entire jar while mulling over the meditator's tirades. Not a huge jar, mind you, but even so. And also a mini-bundle of flutes with various little cheeses flavored with cumin, red pepper, and green pepper. Not to mention a string of sausages scarcely longer than a finger, but nice and fleshy under their pink skin, filled to bursting. A disaster for the *mens sana*, those delicacies that winked at you from the back of the fridge and begged you to take them away from there, where their little hearts were freezing, to the tip of your tongue where they'd be so happy flattering your palate and warming your blood. (*And what about when we have to send King Lear to feed the maggots?*) There was the fortuneteller again, and that refrain of calumny tossing its sour notes into the magnificat of little pleasures. A sinister solo that could give you goose bumps and poison the taste of the nibbled delicacies. (*If death's terrifying aspect were attributable to the idea of non-being, we should feel a similar terror when thinking of the time when we didn't yet exist.*) Quick, quick, a little something to chew, any old thing to pick on. Just so long as it distracted the choppers and occupied the brain. When Southpaw began force-feeding you a spoonful or two of her fussy-gloomy infusion, you knew you were in for some mental torture, with her voice that grated like a rusty crank and the words that emerged from her grimoire like the jaws of a vise to catch your head and squeeze and squeeze, and pour their corrosive acid into your mouth, nose, and eyes. Blecch! Blecch! The witch and her lethal brew, as Theo would say. *That* one was another thorn in her side. If only he would take a powder one day without warning. If only Southpaw, instead of poisoning the atmosphere with her sinister propaganda (*we should feel a similar terror when thinking of the time when we didn't yet exist*), would aim her incantations toward the attic studio where, at that very moment, the enterprising Theo must have been lounging on the futon, eyes glued to the magic porthole, mouth stuffed with peanuts, and shouting at every penalty call. A little conjuration above the futon, just to see. A whirlwind of scouring powder, a purple cloud, and in place of the eternal Theo she'd have a tabby licking its fur and watching the ball fly back and forth across the magic porthole. Having accomplished the metempsychosis of Theo Senior, she'd need only to bring the unbewitching philter to a boil and down it in one gulp, sending it to the pit of her belly where it would gently shrivel Theo's seedling, wilting it like an over-watered houseplant. And then, no more bother. Happy days would be here again. The tummy would stop threatening to swell. On the futon, the tabby would play with the other, previously adopted furball. The attic studio would see plenty more toms as well. A whole black, white, red, and tiger-striped clutter that would shed fur everywhere, roll on the futon, and constantly rub up against her long nude legs, for which every grimalkin on earth would give up his soul—thus meowed Theo, turned into a nice pussycat.

Nice pussycats she had nothing against. Fur, on the other hand, gave her asthma. And the reek of cat piss clinging to her sheets, hair, clothes, skin: that really wasn't her cup. Even the food started smelling of tom. The whole business evidently had its charms, judging by all those hotties who cancelled their partner's contract, tossed him *manu militari* into the hallway, and remodeled the love nest into a refuge for strays. But playing the earth mother with her train of meow-meows—not really her thing. My elder cousin, emerging from the commode, shot off another arrow, seemingly aimed at no one in particular, while tossing on the table the newspaper brought with her and read in the privy. The paper was a Vietnamese gutter rag, a tattered cabbage leaf, planted on the quick, grown in exile, tended catch as catch can by an army of shadow gardeners. They came to duke it out with the Communists who were bleeding the old country white and to report on the abyss, the nation ransacked by the Reds, wrapped in barbed wire by the Reds, irrigated with rebels' blood by the Reds, then sold off piecemeal to sinister sharks by the same Reds who had now turned coat. Once a month, the cabbage leaf spoke its piece to the tyranny that had recapitalized itself as a limited liability society. The fact was, overnight the shadow gardeners, who'd valiantly crossed swords with the fanatics of purity and assembly-line brainwashers, had suddenly found on the tips of their pitchforks nothing more than a smattering of harried profiteers. Pidgin English had replaced Party jargon almost seamlessly. The Ills of Communism cured by payments under the table! The imprecators of the cabbage leaf were all in a tizzy. Now what? All that for *this*? Ah, if only we could return to that bronze age, to the malignant decade when exiles bewailed their martyred homeland, when they gathered to hear readings of a lament written by some luckless brother in his own blood as he was tossed from jail to jail. Which lament, copied over in minuscule characters on onionskin, folded and refolded until it fit in the palm of your hand to be hidden in a pound of black tea, had slipped over the border right under Uncle Ho's nose. Gone were the tragic years when, huddled in secret for a knightly vigil (accompanied by wine and dishes prepared in remembrance of the homeland), the synod of imprecators listened, clucking their tongues and shaking their heads in dismay, to reports from the old country, which was subsisting on roots, drinking pond scum, and perishing of dysentery. These days, when an imprecator met another imprecator in the offices of the cabbage leaf, what could they say to each other about the homeland's new offspring—those lucky brothers nourished on fine foodstuffs, gorged on succulent fare, who acted fussy and talked of going on a diet but snacked all the livelong day on goodies that melted in your mouth not in your hand, proffered by pin-ups posted on the auctioned walls? Behind those pin-ups who popped chewing gum, waved disposable hankies, sprayed contraband perfume behind their ears, and emerged from peripatetic telephones like water lilies from the speculative sludge; behind those pin-ups, who donned traditional garments to show the barbarians the charm of a sybaritic sojourn in the refurbished palace with its remnants of colonial splendor, its reeducated (not brainwashed!) personnel, its chameleonesque chef who could satisfy any craving, even a sudden yen for a good slab of charred meat with matchstick fries (*after all those chinoiseries in gluey sauce*); behind those spotlit pin-ups who batted their come-hithers at the hoi polloi—behind all that, the hastily whitewashed walls still bore traces of the malignant decade, of commandments to be followed on pain of deportation to former battlefields as a human mine detector. Beneath the ads, the palimpsest of terror.

Which the sentinels from the cabbage leaf insisted on keeping alive. For the good of their numbskull brothers, lured by these temporary concessions and all too eager to forget the decade of barking, when the loudspeakers vomited their red bile, when the walls of the homeland dungeon were covered in banners proclaiming the arrogance of the new lieutenants in bloody characters stamped with the Party star. For the comrades from the North had made it their duty to evangelize to their ignoramus brothers, to liberate the souls they had pawned to the nuncios of capital, to forge them a path by pruning a few heads, which were marinated in the juice of self-criticism before being broiled on a skewer planted at the entrance to one of those academies established in some malarial backwater for the radical cure of thick wits. And now that the pin-ups' smiles, winsomely beaming from the arches, had conjured away Bluebeard's castle, the crafty brothers wanted to forget about the whole thing, the bloody mist over barbed wire, the severed heads, siphoned brains, carcasses rotting on their feet, ankles chafed to the bone by rusty shackles on short chains: everything the imprecators of the cabbage leaf hadn't known personally, but that they reiterated with the inexhaustibility of fanatical windbags, turned inside-out at the sight of their brothers suddenly having it so easy, as if the birds' nests would drop fully cooked into their mouths. Those greedy bastards had made it through the red leprosy, and now thought only of skimming off a few sapèques, reserving their crumb of comfort, and acquiring all the ultra-modern gewgaws with which their runaway brothers, banished to the far end of the world, had feathered their nests—nests that they fully insured and photographed from every gleaming angle to mail to kith and kin back in the old country, so they could dream of tomorrows singing in high fidelity in a kitchen equipped with rumbling range hood, blaring telephone, and deliciously slick picture box. The imprecators of the cabbage leaf fell over backward, seeing that their scheming kith and kin had turned their tottering palafittes into sparkling little jewel boxes tarted up with all the latest comforts, imported and imitated in defiance of any copyright on happiness. Even worse, they had grown impertinent. In the evenings they congregated in rancid watering holes to applaud a stream of loudmouthed parasites, touring comics who made sport of the valorous runaway brothers. Ensconced on the far side of the world, those runaway brothers had once launched imprecatory torpedoes against Bluebeard's ramparts, but now returned by the boatload to bail out the ship. (*Sharks off the port side!* cried the mateys at the tables.) The new benefactors had arrived and paraded around the upper deck, kept on a leash by their motorized luggage and out of breath by the dring-drings blaring from their mobiles, loudly broadcasting some juicy killing to the world. (*Pirates off starboard!* shouted a lookout from the rear of the watering hole, bringing down the house.) They paraded, those new benefactors, ready to talk turkey with Bluebeard, the Ogre of the Mountain or the ferocious Tiger with the Heart of Crystal (as you like), to get their hands on the ancient chambers and antechambers of death and, with a snap of the fingers, transform them into deluxe caravanserais. *Vermin and chosen first!* guffawed the oarsmen, though they left before the end because the next morning they'd have to start rowing early for the new benefactors, who paraded around while dropping little bills, the real kind, the ones from the far side of the world, and not Bluebeard's funny money that looked like those fake chits they burned on altars to the dead. They thought about the dead too, those new benefactors; they required room to build, room to spread out, room to be served, room to drink themselves silly, room to rest in peace. For the runaway brothers, now filled with remorse, wished to bequeath the old country their cysts and sores, cankers and pustules, thromboses and ulcers. So that the homeland might turn a profit from all that lard slathered in exile, all those pocketbooks stuffed to bursting then ruined by luxuriant fare. They had returned, lured by advertisements promising to unearth for them a choice spot on the toniest avenue of recumbent bodies, a bed with a canopy of shrubs, delicately flowered alleys, carved marble slab blessed by the god of the rich, who always managed to squirm his way out of a tight corner, go figure. In exchange for a small wad of green clippings, the benefactors received the assurance that the instant they turned gamy their precious carcasses would be freighted back to the old country and lowered into their hand-selected hole in the ground, not to mention saluted by wails from a volley of mourners hired for the occasion. A pantomime by monks or a priest, a few moans and mumblings at the edge of the pit, and the lips of marble would shut upon the inestimable putrid flesh of the aforementioned benefactors. For now, the inestimable flesh reaped the benefits. The pin-ups hovered over the benefactors' berths to offer them a flashy seaside villa, or maybe a jalopy repainted like new with stylish escort, or maybe plaintive zithers to accompany fits of melancholy, or maybe an evening of shaking their booties on a small, brightly lit cruise ship, lurching in the footsteps of slender lianas who'd been broken by the malignant decade and were now thrown like nestlings into the serpents' pit. The serpents hissed, and immediately the pin-ups peeled themselves off the walls and bent over backward to please them. The serpents insinuated themselves into the tiniest corners, spurred on by their victorious ringtones; affectless vipers sounding their death rattle, they poisoned everything. The rattlers had entered the castle. They slithered up to the feet of Bluebeard, who had opened only the seventh chamber for them, which he'd unloaded cheap, and now they were crawling about everywhere, hissing the song of temptation in every direction. They had slinked even up to the master's bed, where they waited to deliver the fatal bite. Bluebeard awoke one morning with a knot of rattling snakes in his chambers, *dring-dring time for the final raid.* The castle had been infiltrated from rafters to basement, the dungeons transformed into bright display windows where the rattlers lounged on the highest branch of the nugget tree. Bluebeard had no choice but to cry counterrevolution, order the pin-ups' smiles to be taken down and the walls of the castle papered with warnings against the insidious subversion. The informers found their voices again, the peons hissed the return to virtue, the purifiers cleansed the air of capitalist miasmas—all to the great joy of the exiled imprecators, who had predicted this return to the cudgel. The numbskull brothers were dumbstruck. They'd thought Bluebeard had changed into an avuncular old chief, glad to recycle his dungeons into prosperous bazaars for the joy of his children. And here the castle was ringing anew with the roars of that same Bluebeard, who had bolted all the exits, reopened the ergastula, and unleashed a pack of hounds to fall upon his children, shake them by the scruff of the neck, and smash them against the wall. Bluebeard sent his hounds to the market to trash all that counterrevolutionary junk. They pawed through the bins, tore down the ads, kicked over the stalls, made off with the good stuff and trampled the rest, and barked at the signs inspired by the latest decadence. On the far side of the world, in the offices of the cabbage leaf, spirits ran high. The imprecators shook their fists in unison, lamented in concert the fate of their brothers, so buffeted by conflicting waves, never safe from the hurricane. According to the latest bulletins, Bluebeard's pack was harassing an old poet, who could only see out of one eye after spending the malignant decade in Bluebeard's second chamber, the one that specialized in tracking down the propaganda agents of a degenerate culture. The scrawny old man's one good eye opened one morning to the sight (removed from view several lunations ago so as not to scare off the visiting greenhorns) of baying hounds invading his house, shredding his books, and carrying off his manuscripts in their chops. The scrawny old man's one good eye had seen it all before and shed nary a tear at the ransacking of his garden. But when the news reached the far side of the world, the imprecators at the cabbage leaf released a flood of protests about the fate of the old poet in his skiff, buffeted by conflicting waves, never safe from Bluebeard's sneezes, now that he had roused himself from his good-natured slumbers and was pacing around his watchtower, goaded by a new hankering to inflict pain. The terror returned full steam ahead, to the great pleasure of the imprecators in exile, who had predicted this return to paranoia. No one would ever hoodwink them into fraternity. Bluebeard kept deploying his instruments of torture. Wasn't he brandishing one now, all shiny and cutting-edge? And the imprecators watered their cabbage leaf with desolate ink, which drooled in indignation as it spread the horrific news: Bluebeard was castrating his offspring. For at bottom, it was a mass disemboweling, an attempt at assembly-line sterilization hiding behind the modest proposal advanced at the last hound convention to prevent the children of the poor from proliferating. To all the slackers who did nothing but sit around and spread their seed, Bluebeard offered a free vasectomy, immediate sterilization, granted gratis, and compensated with a bonus for heroism, the amount of which (a pittance, paid in revolutionary coin) might even be doubled, depending on whether the guinea pig exited the lab head high or feet first. The same plenum had addressed the market for rugrats, where the benefactors from the far side of the world came to do their shopping *dring-dring wouldn't it be marvy to buy ourselves a lice-ridden tadpole and take it to the wonderland where people fart into silk dring-dring and teach it to sit up straight hands on the table eyes lowered mouth shut heart heavy with gratitude.* The market earned a ton. But each rugrat weighed, wrapped, and bagged was another gob of spit on Bluebeard's face, and he wouldn't rest until he'd stemmed the proliferation of tadpoles— a quandary that his hounds, mindful of the just man's slumber, had resolved by promising a revolutionary bonus to each guinea pig who volunteered for the snip-snip that would spare him the bother of paternity. The cabbage leaf trembled with rage and pity as it spread the news. Bluebeard opened his castle to pinheads from the far side of the world, invited them to come lounge in cozy dwellings with a view of the mist-shrouded bay, the coconut-lined seashore, the secular temple, the flower stalls, the rumbling construction sites where they built dizzying skyscrapers designed to absorb whole rashers of pinheads, refreshed, tucked in, feted, shuttled around from bay to beach, temple to building site—and all this time Bluebeard was devouring his offspring, castrating his sons, and dispatching his pack of hounds to the homes of old poets. The cabbage leaf writhed in agony as it recounted in minute detail the miseries the old poet was made to suffer. In his honor an imprecatory editorial was concocted, the preamble to a wine-tasting that gathered the synod of imprecators who all knew the score: paradise was artificial, the opening of the castle a booby trap for the captive brothers, and Bluebeard's benevolent somnolence a prodrome of nightmares for his children's nights and days. The imprecators practically choked on their wine-drenched imprecations. The cabbage leaf shuddered in horror, ear to the ground, straining to hear the mournful echo of this latest turn of the screw, every little creak of which was noted, recorded, and briskly reported between two ads (the cabbage leaf had to be fertilized, after all) luring a convoy of suckers toward Bluebeard's castle, an all-inclusive discount package tour, with a plunging view on idyllic stage sets—set up and taken down as need be—and custom-tailored foodfests, guaranteed antiseptic, free of tapeworms and flavor. But those ads were aimed at barbarians who wanted to treat themselves to a modest pit-a-pat by dipping their toes in the anthill that had suffered so and was valiantly lifting its head again. For the exiles, the cabbage leaf had a different set of ads, offering low round-trip fares that would let them witness up close the latest turn of the screw that was strangling their brothers, no sooner released by the hounds than already seized again. The prodigal sons returned. Trussed up in their marked-down designer suits, they trailed behind them their shock-proof suitcases wobbling on exhausted wheels, and a whole electronic arsenal, hypersensitive machine guns already pointed at the wonders of the old country and poised to salute with a Fujicolor salvo the kith and kin they'd left stranded. They returned with their coddled offspring who didn't catch a word of the country's queer lingo, especially when the same word walked a tightrope of meanings—mother, or ghost, or horse—a whole ballet of avatars, depending on whether the accent leaned one way *má* or the other *mà*, or yo-yoed around the word, dabbing a beauty mark under the chin *mạ* or a flopped question mark on the forehead *mā*. The offspring coddled in the berth of exile offered an eyeful to the lice-ridden brats, whose bare feet posed timidly atop one another, rubbing their filth, wiggling their toes, rising on their tips, and who formed a swarming train behind the princely repats come to stir up the dust of the old country, shod in supple, shiny calfskin, in which the wide eyes of their little lice-ridden brothers were reflected as they commented in their obscure idiom on the fashionable gear of the visiting infantes. But then the infantes, swelling in number thanks to Bluebeard's fits of hospitality, began to see their popularity decline, their gear copied by a few local slyboots who now paraded about, trussed up in knockoffs of the marked-down suit, shod in pleather, towing suitcases and valises made of pasteboard, and treading impertinently on the princely repats, who in any case had no business there, on that soil they had deserted during the malignant decade, leaving the bare feet to stir up the dust by themselves, to pound the pavement and harvest only a fistful of rotten tubers. Bluebeard's castle had begun mass-producing knockoff designer suits, and the visiting little princes, instead of being welcomed and scrutinized head to toe by a lice-ridden honor guard, could no longer take a step without running into their doubles, decked out just like them, making the sidewalks echo just like them with the heels of their identical shoes. Sure, the get-up was perfectly suitable when seen from a distance; but up close, it gave off an aura of counterfeit and cheap labor, poor-quality materials and colors that ran out of fashion. So much for the pleasure of the little princes, who parachuted into the anthill that had suffered so. At the rate things were going, the prodigal sons would soon find they'd lost the starring role — though they could still count on Bluebeard's mood swings, the occasional screaming tantrums that sent him stomping on the anthill. And immediately, as if by a spectacular sleight of hand, the hounds whisked away the grand masthead and the castle looked like a penitentiary again, the sidewalks emptied out, everyone scurried for cover, nimbly peeling off their outfits from the good old days and storing them away. Now they went out straitened in the uniform of virtue. They hugged the walls to avoid the hail of denunciations. They bore their burden stoically, like those servant women attached to the bedside of a moribund old autocrat, waiting on him hand and foot, careful not to annoy the dying ogre even when he spat in their faces, pinched their arms, yanked their braids, bit their hands with his three wobbly incisors, or pricked their derrieres with the safety pin that held up his house pants: they didn't turn a hair. These were the ulcerated beast's final roars. They just let him rant and rage in his bed, spit up his bile, exhale his toothless carnivore breath. Now and again, the sovereign carrion awoke full of vim and vigor. Then he would summon his servants with a paternal voice, caress their arms and hair, rewarding their docility with one of those precious little objects he kept close against his skinflint hip. He allowed them to laugh and speak, to open the windows and let some light into the beast's lair. Until the vapors of persecution went to his head once more and he rose in the middle of the night, knocking over the chamber pot, and ordered his hounds to fall upon the servant women and mark them with their fangs. Just so they'd never forget who was master of this castle. According to the imprecators in exile, the fury of the old beast was still claiming victims in the anthill that had suffered so and that was still not safe from Bluebeard's stomping feet. My elder cousin had taken her sweet time in the powder room to peel through the cabbage from end to end, from the freshest imprecations to the coded advertisements. She made up her mind as she burst from the privy. They had to act quickly, wrest King Lear from the castle, haul him in to the gleaming kitchen and ship him back before Bluebeard pulled an about-face and dispatched his hounds to block the exits. Because then, when it came to escaping to paradise, tough luck! One step too far and he'd be in for the kill; the hounds would chuck King Lear into the dungeon, complete with his bundle and passport. But then, what if, once the old man was out, Bluebeard took a notion to bolt the castle entrance and quarantine the anthill? There'd be no way to ship King Lear back, and he'd have to settle into the gleaming paradise…. My elder cousin tossed out the cabbage leaf along with that awkward hypothesis, casually adjusted her bun, picked up a sponge, and rubbed energetically at an invisible stain on the sink. The telephone started yapping like a lap dog startled by a ghost.

Do you ever think of him without wanting to retch? Very often— rarely—never? Do you still love him even a little? Not really—not in the least—you haven't reached a verdict? Did you ever love him? For the hell of it—right at the start—while admiring yourself in the mirror? Do you at least love him now that he's down and out? Yes— no—you haven't reached a verdict. You yawn. You uncross your gorgeous gams. You stand up, tugging behind you the phone that sputters brekekekexkoaxkoax all the way to the window. You light a fag without putting down the receiver, so as to miss none of the plaintive survey. You sigh, but you don't hand down a verdict. You had no opinion, no pity for Theo the drag who, in a voice frayed by the tedium of a Sunday only half dissolved in dregs of bourbon, tried to sound out your heart and, as if desperate to snap his drill bit on a boulder, yelled, sobbed, threatened to slice up the futon and toss all the knickknacks out the window of the attic studio; then, like a consummate tactician, tried a new routine, made himself all humble, all gentle, all cuddly, fished for a tender word, a droplet of affection (even stale) in his ear, but caught only a long, stubborn silence punctuated by the faint sound of lips dragging on a cigarette. He waited, his empty whiskey glass in hand. The ice cubes tinkled impatiently. At the other end of the line, the pouting lips exhaled a cloud of boredom. In response, he crunched on an ice cube, making it creak between his teeth, those meticulous chompers that had long lost their bite. The pouting lips emitted a hiccup of disgust, not even bothering to complain about the sound that sent a glacial shiver through the line. The cube went down with a glurp, taking with it all the honey on his tongue with which he hoped to snare the heart and lovely plumage of the little birdie perched on the other end of the wire. Theo cleared his throat, discarded his sugary phrases, and huffed out thick bourbon-laden clouds that emptied their acrimonious downpour into the receiver. She should be careful not to push him too far. He could be more vindictive than she knew. He wouldn't stand for being treated like a repressed undesirable ad lib, a second-class citizen condemned ad vitam aeternam to claw at the gates of paradise, an ailing calf sniveling a capella for a small place in the manger and a bout of pleasure put off sine die. Dolls like her were a dime a dozen. He just had to stand at any subway exit to reel them in — and not stuck-up snots, either, but young things who really got you in the gut, pleasingly plump little Magdalens desperate to confess their sins, if only some kind soul would sample them first. They might not have the world's most decorative kissers or legs ad hoc, but that only made them more welcoming, not to say needy, and less inclined to drop you flat once those legs had finished wending their way around your waist. He had known a few like that. Who would wait for him in the evening, between the stack of ironed laundry and the steaming saucepots. Who didn't make a casus belli over an extra glass or two. Who asked for second helpings at night, tickled his belly, nibbled his ear — and if he kept on snoring, they just slid beneath the sheets and, with greedy lips, enjoyed a little coda to the Song of Songs. Ah, the sweet ones! So unhoped-for! So hospitable! The gracious mainstays, always eager for the shaft, never tiring of ardent sallies from the Theomantic imagination! Ah, the big-hearted Cinderellas, with their funny little faces and Pinocchio noses, their peepers that emitted only the feeble light of a sooty candle, but so affectionate, so conciliatory, who washed your socks and worried themselves sick over your inner workings when the full moon interfered—which was only to be expected, given the alignment of the stars that exposed your sign (destined to suffer a slew of enteric miseries) to the perturbing ascendance of two malicious planets; but as soon as they'd moved out of their dissonance with Virgo, Mars would get you back on track, Mercury would take you for a ride, so long as Jupiter retrograding with your Sun didn't gum up the works, because then nothing to be done but let others reap what you'd sown. And even if you were of a nature to count your chickens before they hatched (whether Jupiter crossed your sign or parked his chariot at the House of your zodiacal neighbor's sector), the sweet, unhoped-for, hospitable ones asked nothing better than for you to reap what *they* had sown. Ah, those flatterers, who pumped you up, fawned over you morning and night, hung from your hem and your lips, gathered all the pearls that dropped from your mouth and immediately stored them away, to be taken out later one by one and beaded religiously in the company of their best girlfriends, summoned to the telephone to hear their lovestruck sister in full echolalia blissfully reel off the latest string of *TheosaidTheowantsTheothinks, amen!* followed by *TheossleepingwellTheosputonweightTheoshappy, alleluia!* Ah, those gossips, who wallowed in your witticisms, copied your concepts, stole your stories! Ah, the understudies, who wanted to dress just like you, remake themselves in your image, so that in the evening, between the stack of ironed laundry and steaming saucepots, it was yourself you came home to—in a lesser version, of course.

Who's to wonder, given all that, that you'd grow morose like a collapsible top hat covered in mold, a bon vivant wedded to his killjoy. Who's to wonder, given all that, that you gave them less attention than you used to. Ah, the soothers! The exasperators! The slow killers! Who ran sniveling to the phone to reel off their string of grievances, repeated in chorus by the girlfriends who'd heard it all before. They should all be strung up by their . . . , those egotists, those cads, those satraps without a cent or a creative thought to their name—they were about as exciting as a broomstick and they treated the sweetheart, the wonder of wonders, like a dishrag! And the girlfriends fomented the revolt of the dishrags, who in any case knew the whole thing would wind up dead in the water, given the astral synergy that promised emotional letdowns and the conjunction of several austere planets in his sign, which was said to be devoted under the crusty exterior but troubled, since the Moon had entered Libra, by Neptune that fostered dependency, Mars that added fuel to the fire, and Saturn that gave off wafts of acedia. And the dishrags, blinded by the cloud of stardust, decided it was time to do some housecleaning, give the broomstick an ultimatum to shake it, sweep out the routine, plunk his sweetheart, his wonder of wonders, on the seat behind him and take her out to dance up a storm, even if it was just an attempt to stave off the inevitable—given the astral incompatibility between his sign, which tended toward idealism, and your ascendant, which had the devil in the flesh, the fatal spur, the greedy chelicerae, and always ended up sending it all straight to hell, for such was its nature. Ultimately, even with the so-so's— who should have been content with the scraps that fell on their plate—everything came to a screeching halt. The only possible conclusion was that he was cursed or that true love didn't exist, Theo murmured into the receiver, swallowing the last, half-melted ice cube in the glass. And what about the ice cube at the other end of the line? Had it melted even a little over the prior misfortunes of its soon-to-be ex, who was connected to the terra beata of true love by an isthmus that the acid of promises unkept and the rust of idleness had gradually eroded and corroded? Not a teardrop. Not even the blink of an eyelid. The iceberg was adrift. Her frozen peaks danced as she watched the ship that had run aground on her flank founder. Would the iceberg be coming home soon to Rue Glacière, or would she continue to drift—no matter where, so long as she could avoid the shipwreck and his badly refitted exes? The capsized skipper knew better than to call here, to broadcast the commotion of his foundering over the phone, transmit his distress signals to the spanking new house, which on the occasional Sunday had pulled him out of the drink, caulked his soul, and ballasted his cargo hold. Not that those ports of call were exactly a laugh riot, between Albatrocious with her martyred face and Nutsandbolts, silent as a novice, who suddenly began brandishing his fork at the millions of little Chinese who had plunked their bottoms on the roof of the world and made life miserable for the heir presumptive to the monk-in-chief. It was enough to send you clambering up the mast. But at least there was free food and drink, and the skipper in distress could take shelter from the storm of boredom that arose with the Lord's day of rest and dragged him and his frail vessel toward the fathomless sinkhole. Which is where he found himself at present, he had to emphasize: hearing him joke like this, with a wit born of despair, the iceberg might get the wrong idea and think he was exaggerating as usual, whereas de profundis clamavit. If the iceberg hurried home, she could verify all this de visu. But the phone went *No!* The gorgeous gams strode away from the window to go stretch out on the English sofa bed and the phone, jerking back the way it came, rolled to the foot of the sofa, where its navy-colored shell was comforted by the caress of a delicate pink toe that tapped on the little keys and sent, as if inadvertently, shrill bleeps into the ear of De Profundis. Now even the telephone was giving him the vade retro. Sic transit gloriam! Not so long ago, the voice of the case dismissed could have melted the iceberg's heart. At the tele-marketing firm, between two sessions with nobodies interro-gated until they confessed their preference for canned peas and Callipygian Venuses gone wild, they used to call each other from their respective cubicles, she swooning, he cooing. The iceberg couldn't have forgotten that! Her gorgeous gams used to rub to-gether contentedly when the blower exhaled the breath of the fu-ture shipwreck, who back then was welcomed with sighs of plea-sure as a velvet-throated oracle. But no: the gorgeous gams had no desire whatsoever to return to the ranch. The rose-colored pinky toe pressed the * key, sending a shriek of refusal into the Theic ear, which was velcroed to the receiver so as not to miss any of the iceberg's comings and goings, and which shuddered, reddened, paled at this affront to its bruised drum and tender ventricles. Could she please leave those keys alone, please? Would it be too much for her to respect the nerves of a hypersensitive artist of life, who would never get over having once again backed the wrong horse? Said horse, with an indignant whinny, tore her-self from her indifferent silence, leapt onto her long legs, and gal-loped into the fray. And the Theic ear, still velcroed to the re-ceiver, received a blast of bile whereby the phone bill hadn't been paid up and service restored so the artist of life could proclaim his little misunderstood tragedy at the expense of the princess, who wasn't about to sit there and let herself be treated like some old nag. The princess banged the phone down. In the time it took to light another coffin nail, the instrument started wailing again at her feet. No need to get her dander up. The tiniest trifle and she got on her high horse, I mean, she was acting like a real cow, no, I mean, oh shit! He'd messed up again. But if she hung up on him again, swear to God, he'd hop the next local and show up at the spanking new house. Strong wind advisory. Gale force 9. So could she please, for once, cram a lid on the petty insults that were always about to boil over and show a little compassion, the way she knew how, even now that flies were swarming over the gangrene that had corrupted their love? And don't bother making that skeptical little pout, her that's-just-a-big-word-for-flying-leaps-that-end-in-pathetic-tumbles face. Hadn't he tried to get back on his feet? Just last month, hadn't he taken her to the concert by the Mythic Showstopper, for which a big wheel he was chummy with had scored him two free tickets—though in fact they allowed access to a small square of lawn at the foot of the amps, and not to preferred seats in the press box as he'd been led to believe, nor even to the bleachers with the jostling vulgum pecus? The big wheel was just a big talker: Theo had met his match. But hadn't he, to make up for this latest disappointment, deployed all the riches of Theosophic eloquence, poking fun at the hack reviewers, those little know-it-alls in their outhouse, pissing out oracles while in the pay of the record multinationals, toadies for those little insects called ephemera (the complete opposite of the Mythic Showstopper), who lurched onstage to make asses of themselves for an hour or two, then croaked while slobbering over their faces in the mirror? Not to mention the bovine herds parked in the bleachers who went nuts over the slightest drum solo, even if it sounded like a clatter of pots tied to a mutt's tail. Whereas she and he, seated on the bit of lawn trampled just last night by the victors of the Cup, they had exhilaration, and as long as you have exhilaration, what difference if it starts to drizzle? But genuine, simple joy was never enough for the iceberg, who was freezing her assets off, sitting in a pleated miniskirt on the wet grass. And on top of that, the rain would make her hair frizz. And those amps took no pity on the fragile flower saddled with this twit (omniscient, to boot!) who screamed into her frail and already overloaded ear scraps of his vast science, such as that Tibetan bells and twelve-tone music had had a quite surprising and very fruitful influence on the Mythic Showstopper—who was now making the bovine herd bellow and stampede down from the bleachers to tread on the pleated hem of the miniskirt already soggy with rain, then rush the stage, tromping on the delicate shoes of the fragile flower who had stood up quickly to avoid being knocked over on the grass and mistaken for pasture. Talk about your fiascos! The heavens themselves had got into the act, turning the fine drizzle into a full-scale downpour that left the delicate creature shivering, sniffling, ready to burst into tears at seeing herself so pitiful, with her hair hanging limp and that crumpled rag clinging to her behind, and all that water dripping down her pretty puss, between her breasts, into her little shoes, while Numbnuts just stood there with his hands in his pockets, bopping his head and making faces like a connoisseur getting his rocks off, letting out little hummmhummmaahaahhs until a Tibetan bell, at the end of a guitar solo, rang the apex of pleasure. And the hummmhummmaahaahhs exploded in an aargh! underscored by the smack of right fist into left palm. Only then did the onanist recall that he'd dragged his delight along with him into this adventure. Said delight, washed out by the storm, jostled by the bovine herd, had suffered it all without a word, eyes glued to her little shoes, ears shut to the call of the sirens going yeah yeah behind the showstopper. The heroine stood on her square of lawn, cheeks furrowed by rivulets from the sky, which in turn had triggered a discharge of salt water, owing to a rise in the same self-pity that the showstopper was lip-synching at that very moment for the bovine herd, who wiped their muzzles, emotional as all get out. It said in the program that this was a song of unrequited love composed after a night of serious drinking by his Mythic self, who, just like any of the bovine herd, had taken one in the gut, died a thousand deaths, and still had the scars on his heart to show for it, which the swaying sirens, frozen for 3:49 in the pose of healers of the soul, hands to their faces, smiles in check, goo-goo eyes at half-mast, confirmed with a sorrowful *yeah yeah*. Knowing that the showstopper had rowed in the same galley of lost illusions did not reverse the flood of self-pity engulfing the heart of the pouting sponge, who was drenched with rain, puffy with tears, and praying to catch some illness—until finally she let herself be dragged to the exit, dripping with self-pity and swollen with disgust for the entire human race. In the end, it was De Profundis who got sick, he who stayed in bed with ganglions the size of gizzards. And the delicate flower had let him stew in his microbial bouillon. He had sweated it out for three days and three nights, under the eyes of the cat that wanted its treats and turned up its nose at cold macaroni (which the Theic tummy, on the other hand, had been perfectly happy to gobble down), and watched the invalid fagged out on the futon, wrinkling its snout as if he were some steaming rotten fish giving off that pestilential odor. Meanwhile, the light of his life had flown with the wind, staying far away from the Theophagic germs. For if he had bequeathed her his toxins (and that's all he'd done from the get-go, pelt her with affronts, poison her existence; so he wasn't now going to pollute the bit of fantasy the faltering damsel had left with his geezerlike wheezing), if she had stuck around, breathing in his infected air, she would have dropped like a fly—and *then* who would have kept the pot boiling? A pungent metaphor, with which he had morosely seasoned the dish of cold limp macaroni, offered to the cat but the cat preferred not to touch it. After three days, she had nonetheless returned to the fold, with treats for the cat and a mishmash of recriminations for the old cur—he was *not* to call the spanking new house to pull a Don Quixote who had tilted at windmills and now lay there on his pallet, betrayed, abandoned, starved by his Dulcinea, the bitch with a heart of stone, a cashbox upstairs, and a guillotine between her legs. For days he'd been marinating in his fever, his juices, his bile. And the daughter of the wind cared not a whit. She'd gone off to bunk elsewhere. Out getting into trouble while he was pissing blood, from his nose, at least. But this was super serious, the sink was coated in hemoglobin. A little more and he'd have fainted dead away. There would have been no one there to see him die. Just Mademoiselle's cat, which was just like her, daggers in its eyes, a twig up its a-hole. He didn't mean to trivialize. It was fever, solitude, and despair that forced him into these slips of his tongue, normally so guarded. A guarded tongue—that's a laugh, isn't it? Naughty little words, supervised, constrained, punished to force them onto the path of virtue. Sorry—he was rambling again. Fever, solitude, despair. So much disgrace that he hadn't deserved. And every day, another misfortune befell him and dented his conk. Now he'd lost the right to escort his darling, or rather his executioner, to Sunday meals at the spanking new house. The verdict had come down like an axe. His better half, or rather his killer, had made a clean break. Ties. Links. Bonds. The little Fate had shown up with her scissors, and snip! He could cling to the staff of memories all he wanted, tug at the heartstrings, hang onto the telephone line, he still found himself flailing in the void, over the abyss, like in the cartoons; but just like in the cartoons, if he didn't look down he might be able to cushion his fall. He hadn't called the spanking new house to complain about the love of his life, or rather his Saint Peter, who'd renounced him three times without shedding a tear. He'd called on an impulse. To appeal his case, which, if successful, would deliver him from fever, solitude, despair. For he really wanted to accompany his angel, or rather his Judas, to the dominical communion at the spanking new house, where everyone had a great time, with the nutcase, or rather the Albatrocious, the cripple, the cousin who never ate a thing except her heart out, *bitter, bitter, but she loved that, because it was bitter, and because it was her heart.* Not to mention the hero of modern life, the inenarrable Nutsandbolts, always ready to leap onto his soapbox about the recession that was crucifying Hardware Men and the repression that laid low the celestial inhabitants of the roof of the world, molested daily by the Underhanded Little Devils of the Middle Kingdom. And he hadn't yet mentioned Her Excellency, who saved his life by listening to him with the patience that came with maturity. Ah, the generous one, the nourishing one, always eager to stuff her Sunday table like a goose farmer her palmipeds, feeding even the gander who came limping up after the gosling, and who then allowed himself to call the gleaming incubator to gabble for hours, because, abandoned by the gosling who had turned into a harpy, he was shaking with fever, solitude, and despair. And the generous, the attentive one, busy though she was with peeling her onions for that evening's veal, wept while opening her ear to the grousings of this bird in a pickle, drowning in his repentant brine, and asking nothing more than to brood the gosling who had flown off, leaving him the odd duck, reciting his woes into the receiver that the generous, the attentive one, in tears and busily chopping her onions, cradled between her left shoulder and cheek. If there were no more Sunday revels for him, perhaps he could still reserve himself a folding chair in the darkest corner of the spanking new house for the arrival of King Lear, especially if that arrival were to coincide with Christmas: he'd overheard the gosling whisper the idea of a reunion under the tree to the generous, the attentive one, who could most certainly arrange that, the reunion with King Lear. And as an added attraction, taking advantage of the haze of effusions, the half-baked fowl would surge from his dark corner to mate with his female, who had always made him out as something of a lost father, of a pair with the outdated father, the father who left few traces on her noodle. For Darling, he'd stake his life on it, had an Ophelia complex; she was crazy about her father, the dull old blade, and evidently not about the young phony with his swagger and tirades that could drive you out of your gourd. Clear as day. Just as it hadn't escaped his notice that the generous, the attentive one was suffering from a Cordelia complex, the most sincere, most devoted, and finest of the daughters, the one who always did right and received no appreciation in return. He had hit the bull's-eye, judging from the silence at the other end of the line. The knife had remained suspended in mid-air and this time the reddened eyes were not tearing up over chopped onions. Would Cordelia, the generous, the attentive one, refuse him a place at the festivities? Just a small dish at the end of the table—but not too far from King Lear, so that Darling could be moved by the sight of him sitting there, vaguely lost-fatherish, across from the father regained. And then, even with the ice floe in her heart, the abacus in her attic, and the harrow in her grotto, she wouldn't be able to drop them—him and his vague lost-father look—the way she had sacked King Lear. Especially now that, lost look and all, Theo had ended up actually becoming a father—but that, and he kicked himself for it, he didn't yet know when he'd called the generous, the attentive one, delaying her preparation of the veal with onions, the favorite dish of Robin Hood, who, that evening as every evening, had incisively championed the widows and orphans of Lhassa while stuffing himself to the gills. Whereas at the same moment, in the attic studio, Theo was getting himself reamed out under the mocking eyes of the cat, who'd already sniffed out that something was fishy. All this because he had called the generous, the attentive one, who hadn't even put down her chopper to listen to the sighs of ridiculed self-respect, the shredded Theophilic heart, as pitiful as the cold macaroni mush still sticking to his teeth. She hadn't even put down her chopper. The knife was making its little taps on the cutting board as she sniffled generously into the receiver. He was trembling with fever, solitude, despair, and she wouldn't put down her chopper to listen. The veal with onions couldn't wait. She had just turned down the radio. He'd called at the perfect moment to pick up the slack. After the world's misfortunes, the miseries of that sorry titmouse Little Sister had dug up. After earthquakes from across the world, which had made the saucepan lids rattle in indignation, the topple and fall of Little Sister's ex-idol, who detailed his fractures in a cracked voice. The generous, the attentive one was only a bystander, but she wouldn't have picked up the Theoclastic debris even with a scraper. The whole dynasty in league against him—the white goose and her cock of the walk, the Albatrocious in cahoots with the gosling-turned-harpy. And he, sickly little sparrow having wandered by mistake into the hen-house, got ripped to shreds. And now the harpy, after disappear-ing into the woodwork for three days, was back at it, chewing him out, banging the walls, shrieking at the top of her lungs that he was making a fool of her, yowling without rhyme or reason. The white goose must have been cackling herself hoarse; she'd have to regale her cock of the walk with the latest from Little Sister's titmouse, who was already trying to reserve his spot at the Christ-mas feast. In the middle of summer! The white goose had laughed so hard, up her sleeve, that tears came to her eyes. Poor Little Sis-ter, she sure could pick 'em. Even with her long legs, she'd never managed to catch anything but scruffy weathercocks, top-flight layabouts, but unbeatable when it came to playing you their vio-lin over the phone. A warbling that could tickle you all over. A babble that turned you upside-down. And in the pauses, just si-lence, followed by a repressed sigh, like a little sob, that tugged at your heart. But you don't catch white geese with syrup. While she was perfectly happy to commiserate a bit, no way was she go-ing to torpedo the reunion with King Lear by pulling the sorry titmouse out of the soup. And in the soup is where they were, up to their necks, Darling announced, back in the attic studio after three days AWOL. She hadn't breathed a word of the catastrophe at the spanking new house, but, as mishaps go, this one was a kicker. The weathercock wasn't going to bury his head in the sand again and none of this as-God-wills-it-come-what-may! Because, if they let come what may, there were soon going to be three of them. No use sounding the trumpet or making the violins weep. She didn't want to hear it. If they were in the soup, it was precisely because she'd let herself be swayed by the beatheific tremolos. And the concerto in BS-major, which was strictly end-of-season, had sown a few octaves in Darling's belly, threatening to wilt her fine plumage. The weathercock was asked to kindly stuff his pretty birdsong and move heaven and earth to keep the gosling from swelling into a balloon. He'd said yes. He'd said yes because he was happy to see her come back, if only to cut him to ribbons. It was the last traces of fever, solitude, and despair that had said yes; but he, the hypersensitive, rather fancied imagining himself in the role of papa bear, handy with a fondle and a coochie-coo, cosseting his bouncing baby child who he'd nourish on love alone. And as for the rest, all those practicalities so distasteful to the artist of life, Darling would know how to provide, with a little help from Heaven and a few hours' overtime at the telemarketing firm. He had cogitated that whole afternoon, while the Lord rested and the heroes du jour, in blue-white-and-red socks, passed the ball back and forth in pursuit of the Cup, trampling the lawn of evil memory, where the grass should have shriveled away from witnessing the true colors of Darling's love, so easily bleached out by a little inopportune wind and water. All that afternoon he had cogitated like mad, overheated his noodle, which was still steaming when he snatched up the phone to call the spanking new house and beg, implore the darling, the intractable one, to let him keep his favorite new toy, his little dolly, his mewling replica, who would have her pretty puss and his enterprising spirit, natural eloquence, well-bred tongue, loftiness of vision, and all the refinement of an artist of life. But the intractable one puffed on her cigarette without a word, or else pressed, as if inadvertently, on one of the keys, momentarily stealing the wind from the hypersensitive who, at his wits' and arguments' end, yelled into the receiver that he was going to throw himself out the window. The proposition having elicited from the intractable one only an audible yawn, it was instead the phone that flew across the attic studio and smashed its shell on the sidewalk below.

Crack! Yet another fissure in the great love. Crack! Crack! Strange how it made the same sound from start to finish. At first you carried the crackling torch, then, after having been force-fed a crock by her beloved crack shot, Little Sister had finally cracked up and the great love had spawned only a clatter of onomatopoeias *aye! aye! pie in the sky! hee! hee! bideawee! crack! coocoocoo! mewmew- mew! pish! tosh! yuk! blecch! blecch! grrr! grrr! bing! bang! smack! crack! kaboom! oof! nuts to the great love! let's watch it die!* My el- der cousin crushed nuts *crack! crack!* for that evening's salad while plucking her onomatopoeias one by one, little whistling shards of shrapnel to welcome Long Legs, who had extricated herself from the great love and was back in the gleaming kitchen after the tele- phone clash. Weird how Junior knew how to spur her males, cut them to the quick, make them grovel. All those storms she un- leashed left her untouched, smooth, dry, not even ruffled. All those gods, elected then deposed from one day to the next, and who, in desperation, appealed to *the generous, the attentive one,* as the latest in the series called her, asking her to drink their cup of con- fidences to the dregs. And the generous, the attentive one drank, with the patience *that came with maturity,* as this summer's wash- out also said. She drank because any drunkenness, even second- hand, dissipated the haze of boredom. She drank to gather a hint of storm that she could stir into her glassy sea. She drank because the phone had never wailed at her feet. Because the wall built of chalk and sand, with its armature of Tibetan wisdom, had never let out a sigh of despair, not even faked. And back before the erection of the wall, the great rampart against her illusions and floods of tears, she had always been taken for a ride, picked up for life but then put off on the nearest boulder by buccaneers who weren't even evil-hearted, only absentminded; who navi- gated day to day, rudderless, sailing between Scylla and Charyb- dis, instead of returning to port where she'd waited, raveling and unraveling the net in which to snare them. Then, seeing nothing on the horizon, she'd begun calling upon the costly attentions and clairvoyant verdict of some telephone sibyl, who was farsighted enough to fix the rate for her omniscient pride. At any hour of the day or night, the infallible one would sit vigil at the other end of

the line, hearing sharp and vision piercing, her seventy-eight cards
at the ready, all set to make short work of the trembling, unsatisfied phobic begging to be shown the way, to have her life's partner depicted for her, her parturitions calculated, the sex of her angels predicted—for surely the infallible one would know all of
this thrilling program as soon as the phobic handed over her coin
and delivered the account number of her nest egg. And so, without further ado, and while the meter ticked off each minute of their
consultation, the mystagogue, filled with a solicitude that warmed
the heart of the plucked pigeon, had initiated the delicate one
into the secrets of her soul, her internal harp strings, so sensitive,
humming at the faintest call and weeping at the first bump. And
the trembling one acquiesced to this skin-deep portrait of herself, so ill-treated by those louts. But what the phobic had really
wanted to hear was the infallible one announcing the return of
the most recent buccaneer, who had shipped out with no forward-
ing address—something that in all good conscience the phone-
line clairvoyant could not do, as she strictly adhered to the rule
(run, meters, run!) of speaking only the blind truth. And the
blind truth decreed that there was no future to be had with the
rogue in question, who moreover, at that very moment, was fingering his love hymn on another sensitive harp: a future pigeon
for clairvoyance, to be sure, but (run, meters, run!) that was a
story for another day. Was the trembling phobic thus condemned
to eternal frustration? And if this spelled the end of the great love,
would the unsatisfied one at least know the delight—which she'd
heard was indescribable—of someday becoming pregnant? At
the other end of the line, the infallible one had gathered her wits
(run, meters, run!); the Empress and the Hanged Man, the Devil
and the Hierophant, the World and the Moon danced the sara-
band of auguries, which whispered to the vatic mouth that the
unsatisfied one had to sow before she could reap, the richness of
the harvest depending on the quality of the seeds. She therefore
had to give it time (run, meters, run!) but not expect too much,

for everything disappeared sooner or later. First, to revive her spirits, the trembling phobic should enter into communication with the water that cleansed, the fire that purified, the air that lightened, the earth that gave strength. And if this communion with the elements did not help her climb back up the slope, there was no reason that the unsatisfied one, having tried out commerce with the living, couldn't learn to turn tables and come up with her own spirit through whom she could converse with the shades. Moreover, the clutch of phone-line sibyls, in their sisterly solicitude, regularly organized seminars, councils of love to safeguard all the unsatisfied, in body and mind—she had only to hand over the brass, the mystagogues would do the rest, palming off on the lost souls their cabalistic science of infusions. Would the trembling phobic like to sign up for three days of communion with mauve and ginseng, ipecac and dandelion, angelica and thistle? Or perhaps the paying guinea pig needed her positive electricity recharged, a Couéistic fluid specially priced but doubly effective, which would make the veins of the unsatisfied course with the fetishism of drive and the religion of optimism? Once the euphoric waves had turned thistle into angelica and the unsatisfied phobic into a morning glory, the mystagogues would distill in their vats a few droplets of their obscure science from moonflowers, a dialogue between the Hermit and the Hanged Man, a prediction of the future via interpretation of voice, quivering of pendulum, laying on of hands, messages from the beyond, cosmic harmony, the whole nine yards, where the famished client would abandon, on entering here, all hopelessness about receiving love's radiations. For, quoth the phone-line sibyls, everything was love, beginning with the unsatisfied one, who was too hard on herself and should allow herself a few pleasures. It was the unguent that all the bewildered clamored for—you had to apply it just at the end of the consultation. And their hearts melted. Their throats choked up. Their eyes watered. Their heads forgot to worry about the tab. *Crack! Crack!* My cousin put down her nutcracker and turned the knob on the radio, where a mealy-mouthed madam, miffed at the morose male who had muffled her, maligned the dismasted mate who had set sail. *Crack! Crack!* All that time she'd spent dreaming of a great love, only to find herself here, cracking nuts and trying to believe that this was it— that happiness was in her pocket, round as an egg filled with sweets and ready to be gobbled up. But the shell had begun crazing *crack! crack!* and inside there were only humbugs to swallow. Maybe she should have done like Little Sister, hoist herself up on a pedestal, keep her heart in a chestnut-bur, hold out her tootsie to be kissed, pull it back when it started getting tired only to hold it out again, all fresh and smooth, to other lips, less ticklish but all the more fervent. Or else play with fire and get horribly burned, like their cousin, who pulled no punches (so to speak) with her insane story. And now she gnawed at her stump, ate her heart out, *bitter, bitter, but she loved that, because it was bitter, and because it was her heart.* No one ever spoke about her heart, which she had given, first come, first seen, to her damaged brother. Pure hearts loved tenderly, but what do you do when you are twins? Pure hearts toyed with tenderness, but what do you do when you've got your brother under your skin? The pure hearts were not yet fifteen when they'd been discovered behind their parents' armoire, fornicating against the wall. There was blood on the floor, blood on the cousin's thighs, blood on her lip, sucked and bitten by the damaged one, who had fit his stake into the tight jewel-case, his hands glued to the buttocks of his little pure heart and his starving puppy's tongue frisking the ear, the nostrils of his little thing, from whom each thrust of the pale wrested grimaces of pain and moans of ecstasy. There they were, welded together, armored against the outside world. The dreadnought, with neither fear nor shame, entered the channel, penetrated to the end of the canal. Voices behind the door signaled the enemy's approach. But when the door flew open, when the footsteps rushed toward the armoire, instead of veering off they had continued to forge ahead, his mouth sucking in the lips of his twin. The shouting had not uncoupled them. She had barely lowered her face, to hide her pleasure. It had been necessary to beat them, yank the damaged one back, so that finally the conjoined twins would be pried asunder. And crack! Another great love cloven in two. Blood everywhere, especially on the thighs of the little virgin, haunted for life by the scion grafted onto her one summer evening when it was so hot out—they had gone into their parents' room to poke through their things, try on their clothes while they were out visiting somewhere. They had taken from the armoire their father's blue shirt and their mother's black tunic with large flowers; they had stripped in front of the open armoire, had brushed each other's arms, stomachs, kissed each other's necks, shoulders; they had dropped the blue shirt and flowered tunic on the floor and, still caressing each other, nibbling at each other, they had backed little by little into the corner behind the armoire, the sentry box where the two little soldiers who loved each other tenderly could take each other allegro molto, even if it meant dying in battle. Deep down, they wanted to be discovered, killed together, run through while still entwined. But the little foot soldiers did not die from the scandal. And now, the cousin ate out her heart, which was *bitter, bitter,* and she invoked her twin, who perhaps was *not crazy, not crazy,* but had been put away all the same. Crack! Crack! When you got down to it, it wasn't so bad cracking nuts. Good, simple happiness. Ecstasy at a reasonable price. Love with a good head on its shoulders. A little sonatina piano piano. Too bad if that seemed boring to Little Sister, who liked to stir it up, and cousin, who only had ears for screeching. It took all kinds to make a world. Nutcrackers with robust hands *crack! crack!* heartbreakers with legs like scissors *click clack!* and breast-beaters still catching flack. Those two could purse out their lips all they wanted, they still showed up every Sunday for a three-way chat in the spanking new house, which the nutcracker with robust hands had obtained only by the sweat of her brow. Little

Sister bit the hand that fed her, ran a disdainful eye over all this Boeotian brightness, but spelunked all the same through the cave of the philistines, which had the advantage of always being well stocked, bursting with all those goodies that made your mouth water. And Cousin, who ate only her bitter heart, she was there too, watching the others enjoy themselves. If she stopped setting foot in the new house, she would have nowhere else to go on Sundays (let alone the other days!), so might as well set sail for the new house, where she could play Cassandra getting her feet caught in a bourgeois carpet. The very same carpet that the nutcracker—the ever sincere, ever devoted, very best of daughters, as Little Sister's titmouse warbled—had to dye red for King Lear's arrival, finally set for autumn, which entailed the doubly heartening prospect of rolling out the twin spectacles of gestation *and* delivery for the old man. Yet another spanking new pleasure. The phone-line sibyl (run, meters, run!) had told her so, that after the transhumant grazers and egolatrous stiffs, *he* would come, the strong man, the blue-chip asset. Since the love made of chalk and sand had encircled her with its rampart, she was over and done with shedding tears—such a waste of capital—to be soaked up by casual spongers. From now on, she steered her boat like a chief. And, like a chief, she readied the assembly of her troops and the parachute landing of King Lear, whose last letter, she remembered now, had surely remained in the bedroom closet, lost under a pile of shirts or stuffed in a coat pocket. The letter had arrived in the middle of a domestic pandemonium, a tornado of clothes unfolded, scattered about, sorted, and refolded with the help of Little Sister, who was trying on a few things—not the livery of the well-ordered life but cast-offs from the dissolute days. The short skirt that knotted in back, the black dress that left that same back exposed, the tight slacks that played up the gorgeous gams, and the parade of immaculate little tops that waited only to espouse that shapely shape twirling before the mirror, since their owner, certain of her love in chalk and sand and swollen with tranquil contentment, now looked at them as satanic finery, which would sear her flesh were she foolish enough to go out thus bedizened. Junior rummaged through the closet. Get thee behind me, heavy mud-green suit, ample burnt sienna blouse, mouse-gray sack dress, and oh-so-proper earth-tone trousers. The inquisitive hand rejected all those accoutrements of virtue, purchased to accord with the simple pleasures of the spanking new house. No, what made Little Sister's high beams shine were the olé olé items, the follies from the tumultuous years. Mademoiselle never deigned to beg alms. She ran her hand over the object of her desire, which she pulled from the lot and held against her to gauge its effect in the mirror, waiting for her sister to suggest she try on the mini-miniskirt that had cost the skin off her behind, which it barely covered. An absurd whim, to catch the fancy of some loser who'd gone out to whoop it up before remembering, oh shit!, the candlelight dinner and had shown up, unwashed, unshaven, hands and pockets empty but with a three-hour delay, only to collapse in fatigue, while still managing to spill some champagne on the skirt that chafed the skin of her behind as payback for not having caught the fancy of the snoring warrior. Mademoiselle's behind had no qualms with the expensive skirt that beamed at the mirror, all perky to see itself matched with such gorgeous gams, after having to make do with the company of two timid legs, though fortunately topped by an impudent derriere. The letter had arrived during Little Sister's fashion spree, her pile of booty growing by the minute. She wasn't about to let all those follies lie fallow, while her lovely tanned body, which of course looked great in anything, suffered the daily tragedy of *I'vegotnothingtoputon*. The body beautiful was perfectly willing to let its sizzle enhance the wardrobe of the flighty days, every item of which fit her like the proverbial glove. But one had to press these items on Mademoiselle gently, use all of one's tact, without expecting a thank-you, not even murmured, since beautiful things, it went without saying, were hers by rights. Mademoiselle waited for her sister to compliment her, encourage her to make away with these rags just dying to espouse her bewitching curves after so inadequately squeezing the solid waistline that their owner had seen appear along with her tranquil contentment. The pillage had been expeditious, encouraged by its victim, who passed the torch, buried her lighthearted youth, scattered to the winds these gladrags of her past, abandoned her alluring sheddings to I'vegotnothingto-puton, who applauded this self-sacrifice *that came with maturity* and was quite pleased with this sexy bequest, which the lovely tanned body would know how to put to stunning use. King Lear's letter had arrived in the midst of this pillage, which had stripped the armoire of its flirtatious relics and left hanging only the topcoats of wisdom, appropriate to the tranquil contentment of the ever sincere, ever devoted owner of a spanking new house and, soon, of a little prince—who, with a vigorous kick, had manifested his impatience with the letter, read while Little Sister was on the telephone rounding up suitors and accepting bids for a night out, when the lovely tanned body would inaugurate its new wrapping that gave it such chic. But woe betide the mooncalf who made to mouth the lovely tanned body, which would melt a Mormon but relished nothing better than to leave its mortal pretenders moping, without even the mirage of a moratory interest. Once the bids were taken, the fish hooked, and the telephone cradled, the lovely tanned body had made off with her booty and the letter had remained caught in the folds of virtue, somewhere in the back of the clothes closet.

A bike that stayed in place. Now he'd heard everything! Yet another of those whimsies that popped out of King Lear's brain ever since he'd begun preparing for his reunion with the exiled princesses. A bike without wheels or chains, that couldn't even leave the house. An imported bit of devilment for which the old fruitcake had paid a king's ransom, with money sent by his eldest daughter, convinced that by pedaling on it twice a day he'd be fit as a fiddle and, when the time came to lay his homage at the princesses' feet, he would leap forward with the agility of an antelope. Pending his metamorphosis into a gliding antelope, the fatherly old beast huffed and puffed on his bizarre contraption, which wore out his ticker, made his aching bones creak, and left him exhausted. This in no way suited the Wheezer, who was forced to watch this marathon preparation for a race to disaster. The contraption had been set up in a corner of the blue house. The athlete pedaled and pedaled, rolling at top speed on his stationary vehicle that each day carried him closer to his little princesses. And, each day, he climbed down from his contraption, wasted, winded, his head in the clouds as if returning from the garden of delights, where he'd been gamboling free as the wind beside his rejoined gazelles. The Wheezer viewed all this with an ever more dubious eye, but it was best to keep silent, for fear of an eel stoppage. At least let him benefit from the last eels chosen especially for him, grilled with love for him! Since that cursed letter and its siren song of reunion had short-circuited King Lear's synapses, his neurons crackled with sparks of yearning and his brain now worked only on the energy of a departure to the far side of the world. But it was in the other world that he risked ending up, if he kept pedaling on his diabolical contraption twice a day to go find his bounding gazelles. At the crack of dawn, King Lear climbed onto his static rocket and *whoosh!* off he went to unspool an endless reel of daydreams in which he saw himself on the far side of the world, duded up like his princesses' favorite movie star—whose name now escaped his memory; he recalled only the individual's gangly bearing, rumpled suit, and the cigarette hanging from his lips. It ruffled him a bit, the actor's outfit on the postcard he'd received. His own tailor-made suit seemed a bit old hat by comparison. On top of which, he'd quit smoking to get in shape. He'd have to rehearse before the big departure—rumple the tailor-made suit and get used again to having a butt in the corner of his gob. For now, King Lear, panting like a trainee, straddled his scrap-iron steed that, without lifting a hoof, made him see the world through rose-colored specs. He pedaled and pedaled, the charge rising from his legs to his head, which steamed and steamed. His dome gave off pinkish clouds. King Lear's madness flared, stoked by this sudden delirium of love for his princesses. The more he pedaled, the more the intoxication of the big departure went to his head. And when he did descend from his mount, it was not to see about appeasing the Wheezer's hunger for eels, the only thing that kept him around. Oh no, he dismounted from one hobbyhorse only to get on another. The old crackpot was subjecting himself to a hellish training regimen, not only for his body but also for his mind. Each day he spent hours poring over a dictionary and cramming from an old poetry anthology, to stuff into his impatiently burning noodle a few scraps of the lingo they spoke on the far side of the world. And the famished Wheezer paced in circles, his only nourishment a few declaimed verses: *Demain dès l'aube ... je partirai. Tomorrow at daybreak ... I shall leave.* And all this time, the fire remained unlit, the eels writhed, and the Wheezer chewed his fingernails. Still more of the Great Deaf-Mute's mischief. If only their grandmother still ruled the roost, the princesses would have left King Lear where he was; but the funereal caretaker of stinking rich corpses had gone to join her clients and serve as the main course at the maggots' banquet. Now nothing held the princesses in check. And, under cover of filial piety, they had unbalanced King Lear's mind and upended the Wheezer's sweet routine, which these days was now punctuated with the threat, trumpeted morning till night, of *Tomorrow at daybreak ... I shall leave.* The Great Deaf-Mute had scored a real coup by depriving the Wheezer of his eel-chef, who now thought only of beating it to the far side of the world and spent his time preparing for the great day, massaging his calves, working his biceps, rubbing his aching bones with miracle oil, cramming his weary skull with all those strange words from old poems. The Wheezer was called to assist, since he'd boasted he could jabber the lingo from the far side of the world, where he'd been sent for six months of evangelical polishing back in the day. A few shards of knowledge still remained lodged in the Wheezer's membrane, and he'd be glad to implant them into King Lear's, but only in exchange for some slices of nice, plump eel, grilled to perfection. While the serpents roasted on the pyre, the Wheezer intoned in his croaking voice, *Like a flight of falcons from the native slaughter....* And the novice repeated after him. There weren't many who flew from the native slaughter. Only old birds with broken wings saw the door open now and then. Best to rid the cage of their morose droppings. Let them go fluff their feathers over across the world, so that when they were back behind bars they might sing something other than their gloomy, nostalgic threnody about the good old days, the good old values, all those old refrains that Bluebeard and his hounds had swept from the cage. For their unwitting participation in the grand enterprise of demoralizing youth, they deserved to be fed to the watchdogs, but Bluebeard did nothing of the sort. He even let them fly away to the far side of the world. Let them get cleaned out across the ocean and return to peck out of Bluebeard's hand, cheeping in gratitude for that breath of fresh air. The Lear-bird, perched on his bike, smoothed his feathers, flapped his wings, whistled the tune of a flight *from the native slaughter.* Early in the morning, he donned his white championship outfit, jumped up and down on his frail pins, sucked in his hollow gut, filled his lungs to bursting, and exhaled his grief as a jettisoned father. He smelled the flowers in his garden, which opened their corollas wide to catch the joyful heartbeats of King Lear, so moved at being heard by the Great Deaf-Mute who had dropped into his beak a choice morsel, a huge surprise, a pleasure that would shut the wretch's trap. King Lear acted all proud and indifferent, but he was choking with elation as he stuffed himself with delicacies regurgitated by the blue vellum. The wretch believed in all of it, his resurrection, his emergence from the tomb in which he'd been lying for twenty years. Finally, the Great Deaf-

Mute was sending him the engine, the wheelless, chainless cycle that propelled him like a shot onto a rose petal suspended from the blue vellum, where he fed on love and rainwater, dreaming of his reunion with the penitents who would make his life clover from now on, fixing him up, fussing over him, with all the respect due the Great Deaf-Mute's plenipotentiary. And when he returned to the blue house, having had his fill of pecking from the horn of plenty on the far side of the world, maybe the little penitents would come along, to see with their own eyes the anthill that had suffered so in their absence, and that Bluebeard—as they must have read in the cabbage leaf—displayed as a model of industrious virtue, extirpated with forceps from the womb of obscurantism, raised for an entire decade in the chambers of the inquisition, and tightly regulated with generous turns of the screw. Maybe they would come along, to see with their own eyes the ruined palace, where rain dripped on the bed, which he then had to move, push up against the armoire, thereby blocking the door. They would come along to taste the eels, all the more delicious for having been plucked from the Wheezer's mouth. And old Lear would let them admire the rectangular plot of earth chosen for the day when he would be crowned king of the maggots. An imperial resting place, where he'd have at his feet the murky water of the lake and, above his head, the distant murmur from Avenue of the Two Trung Sisters, named for the amazons of the Red River, who had raised an army of warriors and routed the invaders from the North. They had ended up suicides, betrayed by their men, captured by the enemy. But about feats of arms in the anthill from two thousand years ago, the exiled princesses, who led the hectic life of the far side of the world, cared not a jot, as was only fitting. Besides, what did they still remember of the anthill, after all this time? A taste on the tip of their tongue. A tune in their head. Dust in their eyes. Hawkers shouting their wares. A jumble of accent marks. The letters of an alphabet (they'd had it drummed into them enough!) transcribed by a missionary come from the far side of the world, with a *Catechism Explained in Eight Days for Those Who Wish to Be Baptized,* and a method for rewriting in his Roman alphabet the language of the infidel. O holy man! Who had relieved two little Lusitanian curates, prematurely recalled by the Great Deaf-Mute, of their system of transcription, the better to offer the tropical miscreants, in place of the Empire of the North's sinister hieroglyphs, a suite of modern beauties—identical syllables embellished with little scars, so that one could distinguish between when they sang of love, *yêu,* which weakened one's body and mind, *yếu,* and caused one to die in the flower of youth, *yểu.* King Lear was no longer in the flower of youth. And the more he sprinted on his stationary scooter, the more visibly he wilted. So breathless, so weak, but so elated it was pitiful. Once he'd worn himself out on his restive two-wheeler, and the walls of the decrepit palace had thrice echoed with the threat *Tomorrow at daybreak ... I shall leave,* King Lear would set off to church to bray his gratitude to the Great Deaf-Mute, who had only wrested his progeny from him so He could reunite them in a celestial fanfare. Blow, trumpets, blow! King Lear on his diabolical contraption was flying to the far side of the world so he could bring back, in a balloon, the posterity they had denied him, who would no doubt find the blue house a bit ricky-ticky, a bit strange with its flowers out front and pyre for eels in back. King Lear brayed for the souls of his progeny and even for the eternal rest of their grandmother, the departed caretaker of stinking rich corpses, who had nothing better to do than be reincarnated as a mosquito and buzz around and torment King Lear in his sleep and demand the return of the statuettes he'd filched and kept for many years as the apples of his eye before throwing them in the church kitty. Which had led to the potbellied Buddha being swapped for a scrap of swaddling from the Great Deaf-Mute's martyred Son, a relic that at the turn of the century a church looter from the far side of the world had sold to a madam who'd found religion, saturated with mercury and with a fortune made in the tropics to which she'd run (*just like Saint Francis Xavier,* her idol, whom in the end, ravaged by swarms of spirochetes, she saw appear in *naturalibus,* at night under her mosquito netting). Like a good abbess, she had come *with her girls* to the devil's furnace, just in time to rescue the languishing administrators, who sported the flower of civilization on their lapels, by opening a convent for flagellants, a phalanstery for libertines flogged by nostalgia for little nuns from back home. The scrap of swaddling—passed down from hand to hand after the abbess's death and the disappearance of her consecrated paraphernalia—had ended up in the back room of a practicing Buddhist, who couldn't wait to swap the church mouse's amulet for the potbellied one's smile. The Great Deaf-Mute had nothing to complain about. His box of bleatings contained a relic, even if under wraps, and a martyr in his carnival stall. The faithful flocked in ever greater numbers, the three-god monte prospered, and the Wheezer, sitting in his stall like the Other on his dunghill, scratched at the scabs on his heart and strained his weary vocal chords to curse *the vanity and wearisome nights appointed to him. When I lie down, I say, When shall I arise, and the night be gone? and I am full of tossings to and fro unto the dawning of the day.*

The only thing she remembered about the anthill was the Moon Festival. You ate thick sweet cakes. A square, all white or bordered with a browned crust, with a large ideogram etched in it and, inside, lotus cream pitted with bursts of sugar. It was like eating an official seal. The seal that the Emperor affixed to a parchment, and immediately a soldier groveled away with the death sentence in hand. The white seal was chewy and left a faintly minty taste in your mouth. The golden brown was more imposing, with its somber, inexorable air. When you broke it open, there was always a surprise. Instead of sweet cream, you found a savory stuffing and, inside it, an egg yolk like the full moon. But even with their pretty rounded edges, the cakes were nicer to look at than to eat, my younger cousin allowed, hovering around the plate of nuts. You nibbled on sweets and waited for evening to light the candle in the lantern you'd bought weeks before, because you had to have a new one every year. As soon as it grew dark, the children came out of their houses with their lanterns hanging from a rod. The streets were full of red dragons, green fish, scarlet butterflies, indigo birds. It was like a fabulous menagerie floating all over town, with candles in their bellies. And the lantern bearers sang a song about the moon where a fool lived hidden. If they craned their necks, they could see his shadow on the great egg yolk floating in the inky swamp. It was like a long firefly, that parade of little lights. Sometimes a candle tipped over and the lantern caught: the red dragon spat flames, the scarlet butterfly singed its wings, the blue bird perished in the embers, the green fish flip-flopped with its tail on fire. And the poor little lantern bearers bawled at the sight of their magical animal drooping pitifully from the end of the rod, the butterfly's scarlet wings full of holes, the fish's tail gone up in smoke, the red dragon's claws gnawed away by the flames. All around them the festival continued; shadows passed by the charred lanterns, singing. Something had to be done. The brighter sparks ran home to patch up their lantern and came out again with their scarlet butterfly, its wings bandaged with newsprint. The others, sniveling, paraded their rainy-day faces and half-toasted lanterns, but the wind blew in through the holes, snuffed out the candle, and soon the red dragon looked more like a squashed gecko. Geckos, yecch! yecch! said my younger cousin, spitting out the pit of an olive nabbed from the bowl next to the plate of nuts. Those cold little creatures that scuttled across the ceiling and fell on your arms or your thigh, yecch! There were crickets too. She'd never managed to catch one, but she had a ton of them, encased in little matchboxes. Boys came to the fence of the blue house, slipped their arms between the bars, held out to her a pretty box containing a chirpy, freshly snared and brought as an offering. She had big fat ones and little tiny ones hidden in her blue desk. In the evening she chose three, which she let out so they'd sing her something. But she didn't know what to feed them, and as they probably felt a bit lonesome, shut up in their matchbox in the dark, they died pretty quickly. She had also slain a whole battalion. It was all that little hoodlum's fault, the one who'd never brought her a chirpy and didn't even look at her when they met up on the way to school. She'd heard him say once that crickets sang even better when you stuck them with a pin, except you had to know how to do it, and the only thing girls knew how to do was mollycoddle them in their boxes. So she'd started sticking all the crickets she'd been given, one by one. But the little sacrifices croaked without making a sound and they soiled the floor tiles to boot. Geckoes she'd never touched. One time, she'd gotten one on her thigh while she was playing on the floor. It had come unstuck from the ceiling and landed *flop!* right on the bit of uncovered skin between her skirt and her knee. It was cold, horrible. She had screamed and flapped her arms. The repugnant little creature, fallen upside-down to earth, had just lain there, white belly in the air, its little legs all stiff. It was dead, and its tail was short. Boys often caught geckos, cut off their tails, and then let them go. After which, the saurians, with their silly little tail stubs, continued to zigzag along the walls, but sort of cockeyed, as if they were drunk, or crazy. They couldn't hold onto the ceiling properly, fell off, and bit the dust with their white bellies in the air. Eewww! My cousin, wrinkling her nose, copped a black olive from the bowl. One day, she stopped liking crickets and wanted birds instead. Boys came to the fence of the blue house with paper swans for her or baby birds draped in banana leaves, and when you removed their green plumage, inside there was a very delicate translucent paste that melted in your mouth. What she liked best were the printed metal birds with wings cut from empty cans, red, green, or white wings with brand names of beer on them. For the next Moon Festival she wanted a large blue bird, instead of the red rabbit she'd already paraded two years running—his ear was all torn. But before the festival, Grandmother had come to the house with her beautiful car. King Lear's eyes had turned red like the rabbit's; he had promised he'd join everyone at the seashore, where there were tons of birds, real ones, that flew far, far away. And now she had a cat that licked its paw and listened as she recited the woes inflicted on her by the new little Napoleon who'd just parachuted onto the telemarketers' floor: a lout in striped shirt and flowered tie, impervious to the sight of the gorgeous gams, who yapped like a rabid terrier when the telemice were late showing their snouts at the little inquisitors' office in the morning—thus undermining the ambitions of the ignoble individual, the sworn enemy of apathy, who was very anxious to see said office become a *great opinion laboratory* that he'd manipulate at will and with a firm hand, as a rising statistician, a sorter of mindsets, a modern haruspex poring over the entrails of the dissected creatures whose egos got bruised when no one came to poke at their viscera. The cat listened while swishing its tail, commiserating over the misfortunes of the gorgeous gams, of which it had, from its spot on the futon, a highly enchanting view. The gorgeous gams crossed and uncrossed, agitated by the clinking of the lousy bracelet they'd clapped around one ankle out of love for that other oaf, whose very name raised the hackles of the gentle feline and make it arch its back, claws out, ready to attack. But one tickle on its flank and the cute little critter became all cuddly again, rubbed against the gams, then majestically returned to its place on the futon, from where it could watch the long legs lazily strip off their sheer-colored sheath, walk toward the bathroom, and come back scented with soap and dried with a fluffy towel, then slathered with a thick white coating that filled the room with an acidic odor. While the foam was busy eradicating undesirable hairs and restoring their sheen, the gams did an about-face from the mirror to the closet, from which a parade of short skirts was pulled then immediately shoved back with a disgruntled sigh. *Stillnothingtoputon.* Now it was time to remove the foam, which had finished lapping up the unsightly fuzz and was beginning to attack the skin. A wooden spatula to remove the black-speckled coating and the gams headed back to the shower, then returned, almond-scented, to rub against the coat of the observer, which purred and raised its nose toward the dark tuft nested in the arch of the vault. The cute little creature liked the depilatory ritual, all those blended scents, and the silken cosseted gams stretched out on the futon, welcoming it tight against them, in the crooks of their knees, squeezing its head between their thighs, flicking its tail with the tips of their toes. But for some time now, the ritual had become scarce. The little hairs sprouted like weeds on the gorgeous gams, which went out covered, fettered by jeans as protection against the hellhound that its master, the lout in striped shirt and flowered tie, brought with him to the office. The filthy beast rutted about everywhere, creeping silently beneath desks, slobbering on bare legs, jamming its muzzle under skirts, especially on days when it picked up a slightly acrid scent. What a nightmare! said my younger cousin, for whom the injury of *I'vegotnothingtoputon* had now been joined by the insult of corseting, an act of self-denial that demoralized her completely—especially now, when the warm breeze yearned to caress the divine gams. Which, sad and listless, had let the weeds grow for days on end and had regained their pep only this Sunday, when they had restored their softness and slipped into cutoff shorts. Times were definitely hard for the gorgeous gams. Harassed by the little tyrant's grousing, pursued by the hound's panting, they dragged themselves back to hearth and home only to get mired in Theo-the-pox's plaintive glue. My younger cousin, letting out a sigh that spoke volumes about her misfortunes, volunteered to go shake out the rinsed lettuce in the garden, where a white kitten had wormed its way through the dense green hedge and was now rolling on the grass in the sun.

↓

Just make sure that creature doesn't get in the house! My elder cousin closed the glass door. Outside, the kitten had crept up to the ball of netting stuffed with greens that swung in the waning sunlight, sending a fine spray onto the blue ballet slippers and the long bare legs. The kitten cocked its head, eyes following the joyous waltz of the salad basket. The flying droplets tickled its nose leather. It raised a paw, rubbed its nose, and swatted at the ball, which suddenly stopped dead. Startled, the kitten bolted across the lawn. My younger cousin opened the door a crack, set the basket on the tiles, and turned back to the kitten. She called to it, squatting, her hand stretched toward the frightened little white ball that backed toward the yellow shrub at the far end of the garden. Two bells had rung simultaneously in the kitchen, making its occupant jump; she dropped the salad bowl, banged on the lunatic old oven to make it shut up, then hurried into the dining room where the telephone was pealing at the foot of the sofa. De Profundis the bone-chilled pretender had wandered for an hour in search of a working phone booth and, agitated, feverish, was now requesting a last-ditch audience *quick, quick, he only had three coins left* with the divine gams—who, called to from the window with the dark curtains, flat out refused to come to the phone and leave off dancing a gavotte with the terror-stricken kitty, which was not allowed in the spanking new house. *Cats get into everything, they shed fur that makes you itch and gives you asthma.* De Profundis cast back into his abyss, the telephone returned to its proper place near the dark curtains, my elder cousin, back at her post by the sink, arranged the lettuce in the salad bowl while mulling over her aversions, eyes fixed on the frolicsome pair scampering around each other on the grass. *Cats are smooth, they slink between your legs and smother you.* And the devil coiled up under their pelt to sneak into your house just when you thought it was safe. He crept in silently on velvet paws and suddenly there he was before you, with his black or white coat, feline smile, and angelic mewing. Time was when she was very fond of cats, especially tiny little newborn ones. She had brought one home once, when they still lived with Grandmother in Lady Jackal's den, the big gloomy apartment near the forest. She'd come home with a white kitten, just like that little demon leaping about outside on the lawn, running back and forth beneath the mischievous fork of the caressing gams. In the Jackal's den, so somber with its lowered shutters and dark furniture, the little ball of fur gave off a seraphic glow. Little Sister had clapped her hands. Southpaw—who wasn't Southpaw back then, and whom they'd shipped off to Grandmother's to keep her away from the rutting dhole, the twin gone mad—Southpaw had been speechless with delight. But the Jackal had gone *tsk tsk, get behind me Lucifer.* They slinked between your legs, they mewed like angels, and they soiled everything, shed fur like there was no tomorrow, put their paws everywhere, shredded whatever they could get their claws on, pissed in every corner, rolled around in a ball, devoured you with their eyes, waited to feed on your corpse, dropped a whole litter just to create the devil's own rumpus and have help eating you up. *Tsk tsk, get behind me Lucifer.* The Jackal wanted none of that in her den. No choice but to bring the little white furball into the forest near the big gloomy apartment and abandon it in the woodcutters' clearing. If it didn't get crushed by a falling tree, that meant it had the instincts of a feral cat, made for hunting, feasting on blood rather than Meow Mix— so whispered the Three Fates to each other as they trotted toward the forest, pursued by the Jackal's yelping. *Tsk tsk, death unto thee Lucifer.* It was dark and cold in the forest. The little white ball was solemnly abandoned on a woodpile after receiving the sacraments from the Three Fates who, with grave faces, petted its fur, then went back to suckle on the Jackal's gall. It was a little white ball just like the one capering outside on the lawn, its fright forgotten. It batted its paw at the clematis on the neighboring wall, then, battle-weary, returned to prowl around the blue ballet slippers. Little Sister murmured to it, gave it cuddles, and the sun haloed them with its dying rays. How idyllic. As if no one remembered the dark forest, the icy wind, the white cat abandoned on the woodpile, and the Three Fates who had rushed off, plugging their ears so as to hear neither the silence of the forest nor the silence of the demon that had watched them run away, mute as a stump. *Dring, dring.* The phone started up again. No doubt De Profundis, mouth wide open and ready to wail over his great perfidious love. Southpaw plum refused to answer the infernal contraption. They needed a cordless in the kitchen, so she wouldn't have to go running to the other room each time and drag the phone by its leash to the gleaming table. *Hello? Hello? How's that? Killing? You said Killing? Miss Killing? No, I'm sorry.* Oh, those people who never paid attention when they.... *Dring, dring.* They dialed without looking and didn't even apologize. *Dring, dring.* This could drive you nuts. *Hello! No, I said, there's no Miss Killing here.... How should I know?... Call information. That's what it's for.... What's that?... I have a charming voice, do I? So glad to hear it.... Come again? Chance sometimes plays such disconcerting symphonies? Ha!... What's that?... Two hearts in harmony? Huh!... Ah, so you like clear, intelligent voices. Huh!... Women with brains.... So glad to hear it. You'll forgive me, but brains are what I'm making for dinner. With vegetables on the side. Which by the way I'm about to go peel. So I hope you won't mind if I leave you to play your little music of chance as a solo.* Oh, those telephone Casanovas! They pretend to get a wrong number, latch onto you, and you're in for the whole moonlight serenade. Still, nothing wrong with a little fresh air on a Sunday, you just had to cut it short before things turned weird. As long as you weren't dealing with a pervert, an obsessive, or, worse, one of those chronic anxiety cases who stammered *please, I beg you, don't hang up,* then didn't say another word, suffocating at the other end of the line before blurting out that they were afraid to die, that they wanted to talk to someone just one last time, hear one last human voice. They'd call their ex, but she'd just hang up on them or unplug the phone. Before reaching you, they'd tried a whole slew of numbers at random. Each time, they got the beep of the answering machine or the whistle of the fax, or else the phone rang in a horrible void that mirrored the void of their heart, the desert of their life. In a panic, they had left messages on machines, distress calls, so that those contented voices, all wrapped up in their smug *we're not here right now,* would choke in confusion, smothered by the chorus of lost souls. The contented voices didn't give a hoot about lost souls. You needed lost souls in this vale of tears — to hear them tell it, the chirpy voices *we're not here right now* were becoming even more warbling, nestled in their magnetic comforter. But you, who answered, huddled behind the shield of *who goes there?* like a sentinel on the watch, trembling that you might be stripped of your spanking new happiness; you who were there in your gleaming kitchen, scraping dwarf vegetables produced by organic farms, doing your best with those twisted carrots, stringy turnips, and pale zucchini served with lamb's brains, unseasoned to preserve the flavor of the slaughterhouse; you who had your ear glued to the rattling radio that sponged up with platitudes the rivers of blood flowing from the Great Slaughterhouse of the world — wouldn't you like a slice of lost soul, marinated in bitters and drizzling anxiety into the receiver? The slice of lost soul was pale with terror, thrashing like a hare in its agony, and it asked you, begged you to layer it in creamy sauce, to feed its desire for consolation, just for a few minutes on the telephone, just long enough for the lamb's brains to steam. Standing at the gleaming counter littered with peelings that smelled of horse manure, you artfully arranged the Lilliputian vegetables, ripped from the wholesome earth, stuffed with organic fertilizer; and, all the while monitoring the cooking of the brains (from the little baa baa who, before being bled and eviscerated, had royally feasted on pure grass), here you are letting your brains be polluted (yours, not the ones from the little baa baa) by these anonymous gusts of anxiety spewing from the receiver. But it was evident that the chronic neurotic at the other end of the line had been placed on your karmic path so you could give him something. You therefore had to lend a compassionate ear to the abandoned one in his vertigo, who was seeing sparks, then saw nothing but a black hole, could barely stand on his legs, clung to the wall, to the phone, to you, who had to hear him out. Well, it would at least make for a topic of conversation that evening, when it came time for the tête-à-tête with the other half of *us*, who'd scarf down his share of brains and crunch his ration of carrots in a silence that could make the walls weep. The chronic neurotic knew the rundown. The scintillating adventure of wedlock. When the *agape* turned into a sullen stew. When the peristaltic compunctions of the other half of *us* inspired thoughts of murder. And what if the fork, which innocently spiked the dwarf vegetables, suddenly flew off the handle and nailed the hand opposite you that, night after night, worried a piece of bread between its fingers? What if the knife, which gently dipped its point in the lamb's brains, found its way into the Adam's apple that, night after night, rose and fell with gluttonous solemnity? But nothing happened and the two halves of *us* gobbled down their portion of brains and crunched their ration of carrots, casting surreptitious glances at each other. *Since when has he had that blotchy complexion? And that way of stuffing himself on bread and butter and smacking his lips in the middle of a silence that could make the walls weep? Since when has she had that double chin? And those new mannerisms picked up from the idler's how-to? Affectations that her girlfriends put in her head? Soon, he'd even have to eat his peach with a knife and fork. Since when had he been making that sound in his throat, like a grunting pig? And his habit of changing, the minute he gets home, into his old blue sweat suit with the red rooster on the chest, a relic of his bachelor life. Since when? Since when had he been there? Since when had she been gone? Since when had some prankster sprinkled the conjugal bed with itching powder? Since when had someone put that weirdo with his epileptic frog face at the other end of the table? Since when had the epileptic frog been joined by this pound of cake, the old sow with no lips and a squeaky voice? Oh, how long it had been that the two halves of us gobbled down their portions of brains and their rations of carrots in a silence that could make the walls weep? Now it was she who wept. The pound cake tasted like daily bread and she had a yen for cream hearts, a pastry usually savored in the fifth climacteric year (5 x 9) when one added a third pillow to the conjugal bed for the big baby one had recently met, an artist to his fingertips who always came up empty-handed, swung both ways, bummed around in frayed jeans ripped under the curve of his buttock, and pecked away, with his artistic and devil-ishly voluptuous lips, at the nest egg in which the two halves of us were so deeply invested, communing for years in blissful thrift.* Would you like some more? The chronic neurotic was suddenly quite lucid. His vertigo had ended. One more bazooka at your spanking new happiness and his fear would wing away from him to swoop down like a buzzard on your gleaming kitchen. Now it was your turn to suffocate, to wobble on your legs, cling to the wall, to the phone; to call the other half of *us*, who was out and about, with a major client, or indulging in funny business with some little chippy. And *bam!* in your face. That's what you get for putting aside your dwarf vegetables to lend a hand and an ear to lost souls. Now they're shitting on your head. Buzzard dung covered the gleaming happiness in ashen gray. O misery of the human heart! O booby traps of compassion! Best to cut the moorings, hang up as fast as you can, before the chronic neurotic committed an acute obscenity, intoning a litany of the virgin bound and revealed in the flesh, her cavities forced into a hackneyed scatophony. O misery of the sexual imagination of bipeds! In that regard, no worries: the bipeds of the spanking new house never put themselves in a bad posture. There was indeed in the drawer next to the bed an abridged edition of the Kama Sutra, but when one had spiritual aspirations and a sense of the ridiculous, turning oneself upside-down, head to tail, on one's haunches, on all fours like a wiseguy chasing his wisegal to bite her behind and toss her on her back, scissors pointed at the ceiling... . No, no, in the house of wisdom they knew how to conduct themselves and they conducted only the most classical variations with hygiene and sobriety. Fie on cradles and wheelbarrows, seesaws and armchairs, on experimentations that shot you straight to the seventh heaven lauded in the annals of perverse love! Needless to say, one did not taste of the other's secretions, and vice versa. Were one to lapse into this gentle vice, one would experience a certain nausea from poking with one's tongue (so pink and clean, intended for culinary excitations) around that cesspool through which the machine evacuated all its rinsings. No! No! You only had to look at Southpaw to see the wages of indulging in mad love. Well before the afternoon when they'd been discovered, she and her crackpot, fornicating like a dhole and she-wolf in a cathouse, they'd already spent their time sniffing around each other. When they came with their parents to visit the gloomy apartment near the forest, they remained seated, pressed against each other, hand in hand, whispering in each other's ears and not talking to anyone else. Even Grandmother, who only had eyes for her jewels, began shooting dark looks at the two wolf cubs, whom they'd better keep a watch on before something not so nicey-nice happened. But even signed, sealed, and delivered, how nicey-nice *were* they, those coitions between coevals who had cohered their fingers to the ring of misfortune? How nicey-nice were those twilight coilings, the rooster making an ass of himself for his daily seed, shrilly cock-a-doodle-doodling his peahen while she lay in the sack driven to distraction? Oh, no, no, no! And here comes what's-her-name from the garden with the white furball in her arms. The beast was hungry, and Miss So-lovely-in-the-mirror—who had feelings, make no mistake—wanted a drop of milk for the poor little thing, whose yowls could rip your heart to shreds. And just then the telephone started bleating again. Was it the chatty piece of work pursuing his rara avis over the phone lines or Little Sister's titmouse trilling de profundis? Really too much! The little prince, roused, started kicking against the walls of his lair. No, it wouldn't do to jump at the first ring. The phone would shut up soon enough, when it had wailed itself out. And there were still some cartons of milk in the cabinet under the sink. But just make sure that creature doesn't get in the house!

Tsk tsk, said the grumpy queen, handing the milk carton and a chipped saucer through the half-open door. Poor little puss-puss, she'd told it to sit tight, quietly snuggled in its protector's arms. Instead it had jumped to the ground and glued its nose to the window, making cuddlesome meows. But the queen would hear none of it and, shooed away with a finger, poor little puss-puss had jumped backward and taken refuge between the long legs, which too had been driven out of paradise. Paradise now smelled of yummy pink shrimp that the queen, seized by a craving for shellfish, had taken from the freezer and was about to peel for appetizers of her own invention. Poor little puss-puss. With a little luck, he'd be entitled to a bouquet of red tails, maybe even a whole peeled shrimp. Meantime, puss-puss and the long legs were banished, cast out, left alone on the lawn, with just a few drops of milk to survive on, as in the stories Gorgeous Gams liked to tell herself when she was just a little girl, at nap time, or at night before falling asleep. She piled the pillows and bolsters all around her on the bed. There wasn't much room in the burrow. She had to lie all curled up, and had to crawl her way out of the foxhole. The entrance was blocked with sandbags. Outside, shots were coming from every direction. *Bing! Bang!* Explosions all around. *Boom! Psheww Boom Boom!* But her burrow was never hit. She had with her a survival kit containing a moon cake, her dozen colored felt-tip pens, a cricket in a matchbox, plus a whole bag of watermelon seeds in their blood-red ball. With her red and blue felt pens, she drew two soldier's heads on her thumbs, on the top phalanx that looked like a little hillock. On the left thumb, thick red eyebrows and a scarlet mouth, like the big gash she'd once gotten on her knee. On the other thumb, a very straight blue nose, a mouth split like a change purse, and calm little eyes like the two pans of a scale. Soldier Redhead and Soldier Bluehead took potshots at each other *rat-tat-tat,* beat each other silly *biff,* *pow,* clawed each other's eyes out *ow, ow, ow!* in a joyous rub-a-dubbing of thumbs, and the winner got to spend the night in the mouth of the little war orphan, all alone in her burrow with her survival kit. Occasionally the orphan emerged from her foxhole, but everyone was well and truly dead, hacked to bits, an arm here, a foot there, guts served cold, an ear in red sauce, bits of brain in a charred nest of angel hair. The world's kitchen smelled very bad. Everything was raw. Spiced with powder. The orphan stepped over the lumps of meat, squelching through red rivulets that tickled her bare feet. The odor of blood hanging in the air appealed to her. She smiled shyly at the emptiness. She felt like telling someone about her life in the burrow with Soldier Redhead, who left a sweet taste on her tongue, and Soldier Bluehead, who always slid from her mouth like a snake. She made up their faces every morning. When she emerged from the foxhole, they took cover in the pockets of her trousers, heads down. But there was no one left, nothing but bone-weary skulls and ghoulish goulash on the cold barbecue. Slogging through the reddish mud, she came across a rabbit digging its warren. It was the red rabbit she had paraded around at the Moon Festival. Its ear was torn, but it could still hear all right. She enticed him into her burrow by promising to share her survival kit, and she kept the two soldiers in her pockets so no one would get jealous. In the burrow, she gave the rabbit a little handful of seeds to eat in their scarlet ball. Then, together, they buried the cricket in a corner of the burrow, since it had died long before; she had left it there so she could talk to it at night through the box and tell it how Soldier Redhead had KO'd Soldier Bluehead. Now that the red rabbit was here, she could send her cricket to kingdom come. It was starting to smell as bad as the crowbait at the mouth of her warren. The cricket was buried in a private ceremony, with neither flowers nor wreaths. The orphan sang him one last time the lullaby she hummed every night in the burrow. She would have liked to sing it now to poor little puss-puss, who was lapping his milk on the grass in the evening sun, but she couldn't remember it, only that it was the lament of an abandoned girl. *Âù o'*, he had gone off with another, leaving her alone with the child. Had poor little puss-puss lapping his milk in the evening sun ever heard such a story? All the nurslings in the anthill fell asleep with the abandoned girl's lullaby in their ears. Peculiar country! The orphan girl had no one left in the world to rock her to sleep, apart from the red rabbit with his torn ear, who listened to her sing *âù o'*, the lament of the abandoned girl. Poor little puss-puss licking its paw next to the empty saucer had no idea of the *dereliction* suffered by the orphan with gorgeous gams, all alone in her burrow with the rabbit who really wasn't very talky. And now, instead of the burrow with a dead cricket and a half-deaf rodent inside, the orphan with divine gams had an attic studio and, in it, a feline much chubbier than poor little puss-puss, not to mention a thriving tapeworm who decried (dictionary in hand) her dereliction whenever she tried to push him toward the exit. The tapeworm who clamored de profundis didn't give a sucker's damn that the divine gams had to drag themselves to the telemarketing firm every morning and get their peachy skin slobbered on by the hellhound, while its owner, the inquisitor in chief, the sworn enemy of apathy, threatened to send the divine gams out canvassing door-to-door in those crappy neighborhoods (otherwise known as the pits of hell) where all you met were slugs steeping in their own slime, claustrophobic creeps, humbugs pacing around and around their empty noggin, rats who'd lost the race and vultures circling over nothing, porkers in undershirts with reeking snouts and depraved eyes, and magpies who stepped out to the landing every five minutes hoping to find *somebodytotalkto*. There was always one ready to fly into your path, grab you by the sleeve, and you just *had* to come see in the living room, on the flowered couch and matching wallpaper, the dark stains *there, there, and there. Who'd a thought the old guy had so much blood in him? If he had anything in his head, he'd a gone to blow his brains out in the cellar, which was clean and empty and made of cement. But no—the nitwit had to be a pain in the ass right to the end and splatter the wallpaper he'd spent a whole damn day putting up. She'd rubbed and rubbed, but the old fart's blood didn't want to come out of there.* You, on the other hand, did. With your inane questionnaire on the joys of being a senior citizen, all you wanted was to scram as soon as the magpie swore up and down that she was *happy happy happy* and that you should put her there, in the biggest slice of the pie, the lucky majority, along with the slugs who spent whole days in front of the TV, the creeps who never said hello, the humbugs who called the police the instant someone rang their doorbell, and the vultures who shook your claw and, the moment your back was turned, sent their crow out with a bar to jimmy your lock. You checked your little boxes and pushed the thrilled, overjoyed, clean-plucked magpie into the wide ditch of those who were so happy happy happy with *this little life and all its blessings,* and you hightailed it one flight up where another magpie was waiting to fly into your path and grab you by the sleeve. You just *had* to see the mynah she'd bought herself when her husband had flown the coop. He'd just finished buying everything he needed to repaper their little cage—living room, kitchen, and bedroom. She'd been nagging him about it long enough. And he'd left the whole mess there with her, glue, cutter, and all. She'd found herself all alone, with *nobodytotalkto* and just the peeling flowered walls to look at. And that's when she got the idea of the mynah. The poor dear was sleeping. She was forced to drape a black cloth over the cage in the middle of the day so it would keep quiet a blessed minute and not drive her crazy with its constant *isthatyoudarling? isthaatyooouudaaaarling?* You checked your little boxes and shoved the thrilled, overjoyed magpie into the ditch of the happy-happy-happys, where she could fly into the path of the other thrilled, overjoyed magpie, who led the same life of Riley, but with a widow's pension thrown in. On the next flight up, there were no magpies to grab you by the sleeve but, from behind the enamel-painted door covered in pre-Raphaelite curlicues, a stridulation to shatter your eardrums: *Love is a rebel bird that none can tame.* You rang, your inane questionnaire under your arm, but the cicada imperturbably continued its vocalizing. You rang again, picking up your inane questionnaire that had fallen on the pink doormat decorated with pale green bordering, and the door opened onto a cicada draped in a long black gown, its neck garlanded in a boa that looked like the blue feather duster with which the magpie downstairs cleaned her collection of flamenco dancers. The cicada couldn't make heads or tails of your inane questionnaire. She was still lost in her art, in her song, busily marching, three inches above the ground, toward real life, which was elsewhere. You checked your little boxes at random, quickly shoved her—her, her curlicues, her boa, and her vocalizing—in the slice reserved for losers and the unbalanced. And while she was still elaborating, in her gobbledygook, on real life and artists *maudits,* you scrammed to the top floor, where you were met by a straw-yellow old magpie and, right behind her, a little porker in a wifebeater and a hellhound just like the inquisitor-in-chief's, chops drooling and fangs shining. Your best bet was to spin on your heels and fly down the stairs without further ado: straw-yellow was the type who trained her hellhound to deal with (by order of preference) foreigners, market researchers, landlords, calendar salesmen, and charitable donation solicitors. Nothing to do but bolt quick before the animals' best friend released her dingo, which was eyeing the divine gams as if they were ordinary hamburger. Poor little puss-puss had no idea of the splendors and miseries of the gorgeous gams. The orphan girl was much better off in her burrow, all alone in the world, with Solder Bluehead bopping Soldier Redhead, a joyous rub-a-dubbing of thumbs just for her pleasure, while she kept score and let out a silvery laugh.

↓

For thirty years she had been unable to sleep. For thirty years her staring eyes had awaited the trypanosome's kiss. Ten thousand lamplit nights. As many dark days, the sabbath of the self, tempest in a brainpan, haunted commotion in the penultimate hour of night, followed by grief at the break of days denied the carte blanche of sleep, severed from the pale breast of dreams. Thirty years. It said so in the cabbage leaf. An embarrassment for the doctor treating the insomniac who had twice thrown herself into Hanoi's West Lake without managing to put an end to her endless days, to the nights she spent begging the wind to blow sand in her eyes, sing her a lullaby, snuff out her candle. Sleep had deserted her the year when the earth in S had been severed just below the jugular S, a necklace of barbed wire separating its head, flushed with Communist fever, from its spindly torso, arched out of nostalgia for bowing to the last emperor and mindless of its legs that scampered before the soldierly foreigner like good imperialist flunkies. She had last shut her eyes on the first day of the year of the great upheaval, the year when the head, sundering the barbed necklace, had tried to spread the Communist fever to its limbs, realign the rawboned torso, halt its groundward rush to grovel as if before the fallen emperor's ghost. Then, once the torso had caught the red fever and rejoined the head, only the legs remained, which were wandering aimlessly, parading for the new mandarins, like polished lackeys rotten to the gills, their sleeves shiny from having so often varnished the boots of the soldierly foreigner. Ultimately, that year, they had eradicated the Communist fever. It retreated back past the barbed necklace, leaving the torso weakened but still sycophantic, the legs wobbly but standing with renewed fervor beneath the star-spangled banner. The red fever retreated back to the head, and that year she stopped sleeping for good, spent her nights spinning wool that she knit by day, begging the wind to blow sand in her eyes, sing her a lullaby, snuff out her candle. But the nights and moons paraded by and the wool grew scratchy as cheap cotton, which she spun while weaving a plan to smash her skull against the wall or throw herself head first into West Lake. She swallowed sleeping pills, ingested potions made from bitter herbs, bathed in rainwater scented with miracle oil, but sleep would not come—neither that year nor the year when, its star-spangled banner shivering in the ill wind, the soldierly foreigner quietly raised his sails, launching the first phase of Operation Go Home; nor even the year when the soldierly foreigner, his ass on fire and his banner in flames, packed up his gear lickety-split, in a whirl of copters and a scramble of radios that crackled about the success of Operation Farewell to Hell. Even that year, when the Communist fever, overcoming the soldierly foreigner, spread throughout the whole body; even that year, when the head, ripping off the barbed necklace, made itself master of the body that had sold itself to imperialism; even that year, the year of integrations and outpourings from the heart, a sop meant to bandage twenty years' outpourings of blood; even that year, the weaver remained in the dark, her staring eyes awaiting the trypanosome's kiss. Ten thousand sleepless nights. Thirty years of drooling with insomniac rage. It was written in the exiles' rag, the cabbage leaf that gorged on manure peddled by the enemies of the people and insisted that, with all those integrations and outpourings, monsters were overrunning the anthill. Before embroidering on the weaver's ten thousand sleepless nights, the scandal sheet had made a great show of dissecting the latest case of teratology: this poor sap barely in his twenties, his swollen stomach aching like a pregnant woman's, goes to see some Hanoi quack. Who opens him up without so much as a by your leave and pulls out a stillborn fetus, weighing barely four pounds, a tuft of hair on its head and fingers and toes all accounted for. For twenty years the poor sap had been carrying the fetus of his twin, who should have been born along with him but, miracle and misery of integration-outpourings, the fetus had shrunk to a tumor and, instead of heading toward the light of day, had taken refuge in his brother's belly. The cancer of Communism! The scandal sheet spun out the metaphor, demanded the excision of the tumor that had gangrened everything during the malignant decade and was still eating away at souls, deluding them with its brief remissions. Oof! Have mercy on the little prince, who really didn't need to hear about such horrors! My cousin laid a hand on her belly. May he be spared the senile ailments of Communism, its fever spikes, sleepless nights, Dantesque confinements, all those stories that could make the hair stand on your head, which was already unhinged by the day's cogitations and about to roll off its shoulders and under the gleaming table, or even farther, under the bed, to hide out and not hear any more about reunions with King Lear—who also suffered from insomnia, if you believed his letters. He was sleeping less and less, getting up earlier and earlier; he sat in the dark listening to the whine of his painful bones. The tardigrade old coot didn't know what to do with his creaking carcass. Not so long ago, he would get up in the middle of the night to go strolling around the city, admiring the colored signs of the sleeping shops in the bright moonlight, like closed eyes that had forgotten to remove their mascara. Saigon had changed makeup more often than an aging starlet with the role of the Modern Girl in her blood, the role she'd played for the twenty glorious years when the theater of war was a dancehall, when one resisted the red fever by doing the tango and the chacha. The Modern Girl swooned in the arms of the heralds of the star-spangled banner, who, *promise me, darling!* would rescue her, *of course, my love,* from the Communist bumpkins lurking in the shadows, ready to pounce on her, strip her of her finery, and force her to wear rags like the militant Hanoi Hannahs with their pinched faces, who made the heralds of the star-spangled banner dance to the music of their rat-a-tat-tats. During the glorious twenty, the Modern Girl had held the starring role, outrageously making up her eyelids fatigued by so many late nights. In the dark, the shop signs blinked their neon and the sleeping stalls raised a corner of their illuminated eyelids to give the passerby a multicolored wink. Then the bumpkins had come, the heralds had deserted the dancehall in no time flat, in a fandango of helicopters

that traced a farewell foxtrot in the sky, cadenced by a kyrie of *shit!*
damn! fuck! like an exorcist's invocations cast onto the pandemonium below, where the Communists were incinerating the naked
Modern Girl rolled up in a star-spangled banner. It was the end of
the glorious twenty and the start of the malignant decade. Saigon
stashed its makeup. The shop signs turned gray, looking falsely
modest and prudish, then genuinely glum, lowering their eyelids
on stores that purveyed only wind, rats, dust, and cockroaches.
The makeup slowly faded. The face paint ran in the rain like eye
shadow down the cheeks of an actress who wished she could die
onstage. The multicolored winks were but a memory. The shops,
still asleep at noon, raised a corner of their lids, gave the passerby
a doleful glance, then returned to their restless slumber. It was the
period when Hanoi the militant, with its shrill voice, dark looks,
battle scars, and drab outfits, met with universal approbation. In a
burst of coquetry, and to demonstrate its submission to the new
master, which had relabeled it with a brand-new name long as a
catalogue of socialist commandments, Saigon (which continued
to refer to itself by its old stage name) had tried at first to adapt its
greasepaint to current tastes, adjusting its signage so that each
shop would hoist the revolutionary colors. They had to scrape
away the thick layer of passé individualism and cover over the formulas of millennial superstition (appeals on the hole-in-the-wall
storefronts to Happiness, Prosperity, the Manes of their ances-
tors, and Manna from heaven) with new slogans that were just as
soporific, forged by the Stakhanovites of the Word who made sure
the ex-Modern Girl displayed her socialist virtues on hastily
painted posters that extolled the Heroes of the Day, waved the
banner of the people, brandished the standard of Solidarity, and
as for wealth, wanted only for the commerce of Workers to flourish following the great precepts of socialism. But the holes-in-the-
wall with their soporific names hungered for merchandise, and every day sunk deeper and deeper into the big sleep. The socialist
veneer faded along with the tears of poorly mixed paint. The ex-

Modern Girl in her militant camouflage choked back the sweet nothings from the jukebox, the *Can'thelpfallinginlovewithyou's*, and rapidly assimilated the vernacular of the Party, bristling with chimerical expressions, *Kremlintovarichkolkhoze*, that sowed terror in the queues, long as the catalogue of a thousand and three socialist commandments, waiting in front of the State-run shops—where, in exchange for a yellowish scrap of paper that had been stamped silly, one received a fistful of paddy and a desiccated fishtail. After a decade of this malignant regimen, Saigon's lids were drooping with fatigue but its eyes were still alert, watching for the signal to return center stage with a dazzling smile on its lips. For now, the facades of its buildings darkened, cracked, crumbled; the wind ached through cavity-ridden teeth; and from the militants' boulevard to the fishwives' alley, the streets all gave each other the same pale, famished, circumspect smile. But the old town was resourceful. The holes-in-the-wall started restocking on the quiet, and behind the closed eyelids the contraband piled up, waiting to satisfy the dormant appetites of the ex-Modern Girl, who strained to hear the gallop of nature, nostrils quivering at the enchanting effluvia wafting from the hundred flowers of capital that had blossomed on the Communist ruins. Black market stalls sprouted like birthmarks on the face of Saigon, which wailed in the swaddling of a new era, burned incense on the sly, and, intoxicated by the opiate of the masses, prayed for the enterprising spirit to banish the last specters of Communism and for there to be a metempsychosis of cities the way there was a transmigration of souls. But while the soul of Saigon felt constrained in its austere casing with its crazed socialist varnish, it had gone too hungry and was too exhausted to reincarnate the carefree Modern Girl awaiting her liberator. She wasn't escaping senile Communism just to fall into infantile regression. Little by little, Saigon took out its face pencils and relit its shop signs, which now announced a soporifically titled creation called *đổi mới*, "new life." But the actors hungered for lines, hastily scribbled in an "up to date" idiom, a felicitous hybrid of eternal Party dogmas and pidgin adapted to current tastes. Saigon returned to center stage and, concealed behind the hundred flowers of capital, slowly stripped off its slough of ex-Modern-Girl-broken-by-the-malignant-decade to assume its new avatar and reemerge as Businesswoman, an undulating little dragon that licked the catalogue of socialist dogmas with simoniac flame, rekindled the nation's heart with ardent profiteering that spread over the ruins of Communism, and sought nothing less than to light a sacred fire in the Pacific, where a cartel of intrepid little dragons were already blowing hot and cold. Saigon tended to its cavity-ridden teeth, filled in a trice and whitened in a jiffy, and rubbed its eyes at the flood of merchandise pouring in. The holes-in-the-wall with soporific names emerged from their slumber, blinked several times, and demanded new face paint to suit the ardor of the little dragon. No more bedtime stories. They had to call a spade a spade, and the little dragon's tongue made increasingly frequent slips. Instead of climbing quietly onto the Communist hobby horses, Saigon gradually started lapping up the blacklisted vocabulary, until, from the militants' boulevard to the fishwives' alley, the streets were nothing but a luminous thesaurus ablaze with the magic golden formulas *fitclubfreeshopfastfoodrentacar.* The undulating little dragon zigzagged between the zip of capital and the zap of Marxism, like a zombie driven zonkers by the years of Communist zealotry, who started swaying to the swing of simony under the capitalist sun at its zenith. Once in a while the Party grunted its disgruntlement, and the little dragon immediately flattened, miming the sad resigned pose it had back when it was but a starving queue in front of the State-run shops, trembling with fear and long as the catalogue of mortal sins against the Revolution. And if that wasn't enough to appease the celestial fury, the little dragon muted its commercial ardor, temporarily dampened its enterprising fire with a nostalgic tear for the years of innocence, the virtuous decade when the shops modestly lowered their eyes at the client's passage; a little tear shaped like a sound bite in which a clown and a clay pigeon, clucking with candor, declaimed in bright moonlight a *Gloria in excelsis* to Uncle Ho; an exudation clueless enough to make you clonk from boredom and choke on virtuous glair. Then their edifying claptrap was drowned in the cloaca of capital, the flood of clinkers that drove the whole clique of mercenary clones, who once perished in the clink but now climbed to the pinnacle and proliferated like kleenex, rainbow-colored butterflies that pullulated on shop counters to clear out the black moths of the malignant decade and soak up the nostal-gic tear of the little dragon — who, emerging from the death trance of Communism, joyously undulated its way to the bazaar of the ephemeral, with its ever-changing signs and its riot of disposable emotions. Kleenexes swarmed across the borders to dab at the new face of Saigon: its fluorescent neons that winked at the mod-ern age, its air conditioners that hummed like fighter planes about to drop their payload, its stucco pilings supporting businesses mounted in a snap, with a rustle of greenbacks that tickled the sharpened hearing of the porters newly sprouting up on the side-walks, sneezing at the drafts of air, flicking away the last scruples of socialism like dust that blended with the exhaust from vrooming scooters and the thick black smoke from factories growing under the capitalist sun at its zenith. At night, Saigon lifted to the inky sky its neon-lit face, rouged cheeks, forehead marked with new scarlet letters, and its somber mouth that, at daybreak, disgorged revelers decked in ersatz despair and white linen: Lord Jims caught in a tempest of whiskey, clutching onto slender, black-clad lianas with strident laughs, their ears attentive to the rustle of green-backs, humming *Strangers in the night* while adjusting the silver serpent that encircled their forearms. Lord Jim, legs wobbly, breath like a shipwreck, sought in the eyes of the slender liana bro-ken by the malignant decade a curative for his nausea with the West. But the eyes of the slender liana dreamed only of makeup

Made in Paradise. And however many misty glances the lovers in the night might exchange, however strenuously they might row toward ideal shores, dawn was breaking on their solitude—the solitude of the delicate flower, who every evening karaoke'd with disgust and fatigue *Strangers in the night, Lovers at first sight*; the solitude of the traveler, with his distress postcards, soluble water-purifying tablets, repulsive unguent that smelled of citronella, and look of panic when an anopheles planted a kiss on his neck. The singsong voice of the slender liana encircled the traveler, but they remained strangers in the night to each other, staggering over caved-in sidewalks where ragged shadows stirred, glorious dregs wrested from their precarious sleep beneath the stars, hurrying to pack up the gear that, at nightfall, grew on Saigon's face like warts which daybreak ruthlessly extirpated. The ragged shadows scrambled in every direction: legless cripples on their ground-level trolleys; mal-nourished munchkins trailing their mistreated mama; one-armed ex-fighter pilots turned into scroungers for cigarette butts, dive-bombing onto sidewalk refuse; toothless geezers, former spies in the pay of foreigners, who'd been stripped of their ill-gotten gains, given a free reeducation in socialist precepts, and then sent back to the school of hard knocks. Still dopey with sleep, the ragged shadows rolled up their grimy mats, swept the sidewalk with their stench of resignation, and, like a single entity, rose to trail the lovers in the night, breaking into an improvised epithalamium, *money-moneymoney*, immediately recompensed by a shower of green-backs from Lord Jim's deep pockets—to the great displeasure of the slender liana, who had cautioned him to throw only small change. But he, the grand pooh-bah drunk on bootleg whiskey, watered the sidewalk with greenbacks and the chirping riffraff *monimonimoni* sprouted on his path like bindweed from sludge. The ragged procession fanned out amid the sounds of daybreak, the cry of the soup merchant, the proot of motorcycles, the rum-ble of cranes, the bustle of hawkers warming up their voices. Saigon applied its daytime makeup, the holes-in-the-wall opened their gaudy eyelids, the lovers in the night danced their separate ways, and the tattered procession clung with all its might *monimonimoni* to the tail of the intrepid little dragon that shimmered awake and pitilessly shimmied off the vermin *monimonimoni* hanging from its scales.

Outside, the white cat was absorbed in his silent contemplation of Gorgeous Gams, who was gyrating her hips and twisting him around her little finger. One step forward. One jump back. A hop to the side. A pat on the nose. A tiny smooch. The creature waved its tail, transfixed. If it didn't venture too close to the gleaming kitchen, it might just be entitled to one of those peeled shrimp pinkening on the gleaming counter, bathed in the waves of *Concerto for the Left Hand* that accompanied the lowing of Cunning Bull, the traffic advisory, as it reported on the Sunday evening roads. My cousin turned off the radio and set her hand to making batter for shrimp fritters, one of Grandmother's recipes, a Sunday favorite. One by one, Lady Jackal plunged the pink shrimps into the mixture of flour and her special blend of spices, then tossed them into boiling oil the way one tosses kittens in a river, while spinning tales about witches whose hands flew off in the night and went looking for souls. Witches and ghosts, that's all Grandmother talked about, my cousin said, coating her little finger in batter and sucking it with a frown of dissatisfaction. Too much salt. And besides, it was missing the mysterious little ingredient Grandmother used to add as she recounted how, at night, the witches' hands came unstuck from their joints and flew off into the darkness looking for a soul to capture. The person caught in his sleep felt nothing but an intense heartburn; but the following night, his hand detached from *its* body to go seize a sleeping heart, then came back and re-grafted itself to its wrist before the sun rose. The hands had to work quickly; they couldn't tarry to stroke the face or nude torso of their prey. For if a witch fell in love, her hand remained attached to the heart of the sleeper and, instead of burning it, it let itself be consumed until dawn, when nothing was left but a fistful of ash. Witches in love never got their hands back, but this was rare: they could only fall in love with their other half, their human twin; and if they gave him their hand, love reduced them to invalids. They lost everything: their hand, their powers, and even their human twin, who never recovered from such a night of lovemaking and descended into madness or simply wasted away. Witches and ghosts, that's all Lady Jackal talked about. They spewed from her thin lips like a farandole of paper silhouettes and danced their danse macabre above the little bowls arranged in a circle, each containing an ingredient, a seasoning, a spice, which Grandmother transformed quick as a flash into a light batter, a perfumed broth, a velvety sauce. The kitchen of the big gloomy apartment near the forest filled with alluring smells, a cloud of aromas that covered the moans of the lovesick witches mourning their dead hand and the incantations of the ghosts, nubile princesses who entered to taste of the embrace they had never known. The little bowls, emptied of their contents, gathered the tears of the lovesick witches crying for their hands, but it was too late—the hearts of the witches had become enflamed over their human twins and their charred hands scattered like ashes in the night, while the ghosts of the nubile princesses escaped from the sugar bowl and spice boxes to dance around fiery pleasures and call ardently for the love that had forsaken them. Their whispers, frozen into pearls of tapioca, were rolled in a bed of cornmeal, covered with a creamy shroud, and prepared for the delectation of gourmet palates. As a prelude to their whispering, they had sung the lament of purification and sacrificed their angel hair, which fell in long, luminous trails into the steaming broth flavored with herbs, served with a fricassee of witches' hearts that were still throbbing with love. This evening there were no witches' hearts on the menu, only lamb's brains, a more appropriate après-meditation. Arrange some greens around the brains and the poor things won't feel so homesick. And, to pass the time before the wisdom-seeker's return, pink shrimps rolled in flour, waiting to be plunged in the infernal electric cauldron of boiling oil and to reemerge in their crunchy envelope, curling up to escape the bite of the three she-devils with their sharp incisors—especially that young one outside who was frolicking with the white kitty (also known to chew pink flesh now and again) and licking her chops at the thought of planting her chompers in the shrimp. The latter sweated with dread in his gilded cocoon, wondering if there were any more surprises in store: there had already been plenty, from the fishmonger's freezer, where the stiff lobsters with their huge claws sneered at him, to the gleaming counter where he lay, shell torn off, legs cut off, head sliced off. Even then, he felt relieved to escape the torture normally reserved for the comeliest ones: they got to keep their fine carapace, slender legs, and pretty antennaed head, then suddenly found themselves perched atop a yellowish mass in the hollow of a green cradle—no, no, he'd rather suffer the electric cauldron and come out smothered in a stifling coat; at least his journey to Little Junior's stomach would be incognito. Junior herself, lured by the aroma of fritters, stuck her nose through the kitchen door just as the telephone started whimpering again—twice, then a pause, then all the harder, as only De Profundis knew how, squatting on the floor of the phone booth, yanking on the cord that was too stiff and short for him to try hanging himself, cursing the three little pests and wishing a pox upon Long Legs—who, cured of her Theotropism, had no interest whatsoever in returning to the henhouse, where all that awaited her was a hungry fox drunk off his ass. Oh, no, no! The little pests would not pick up. The mangy fox could howl himself silly from the depths of his booth: Gorgeous Gams had taken the phone from the hook, cut the line, and let him sink. Strident wails echoed through the spanking new house. My elder cousin turned her little radio back on and the kitchen was lit by a portion of the *Tenebrae Lessons,* soon drowned out by the lowing of the tearful Bull, trapped in an apocalyptic pile-up and counting the charred bodies being pulled from the womb of the blackened wreckage. Then a pop tune took over, asking the musical question *do the dead feel as cut off as the living?* All that remained of the fritters was a smear of oil on the dish in the center of the table. My cousin was mending a napkin, which she kept dropping with a wince of pain, hand on her belly. Gorgeous Gams, who'd left to freshen up, now sat back down, lips shining, her clean hands scenting the air with a fragrance of sweet tarts. She was playing tiddlywinks with some buttons found in the sewing box. My elder cousin reached up and turned on the light above our heads. The white cat scratched at the kitchen door, nose pressed to the glass. He stared fixedly at the three lamp-lit silhouettes, then went off to prowl the lawn that dusk was enfolding in its bat wings. The pop tune had shut up, returned to nada with a flick of the wrist. Click clack! The tiddlywinks flew and fell under the ceiling lamp that swung and cast a distant eye on the book open in front of me. (*We are but chessmen, destined, it is plain, That great chess-player, Heaven, to entertain; It moves us on life's chess-board to and fro, And then in death's dark box shuts up again.*) The gleaming silence was disturbed only by the sound of buttons striking the table, like a lunatic Morse code that irritated the nerves. The telephone started ringing once more. The button, hanging in the air, fell on the back of a hand and rolled onto the floor. The needle pricked the finger holding the napkin. The stitches turned red. My cousin blanched, brought her finger to her lips. Gorgeous Gams bent down in search of the button. And the telephone continued to ring the bells that sent shivers up and down the three silhouettes seated beneath the lamp. Outside, the white cat, standing on its hind paws, belly glued to the window, meowed in the same key, in the pause between each ring. The button had vanished, absorbed by the shadows under the table. The night crept up on the tips of its ballet slippers. The telephone had swallowed its complaints. The ghosts of the nubile princesses danced on the walls of the gleaming kitchen. Their long manes

swirled around the Three Fates and from their mouths escaped
a rueful lament, murmured in the ear of the seamstress, who was
looking for her shears in the sewing kit and, not finding them, cut
the thread with her teeth. The comeliest of the nubile phantoms
came away from the group surrounding the seamstress, who was
indifferent to their song, and went to caress the tart-scented hand
waiting to catch the button arcing in the air. The tiddlywink, striking an invisible obstacle, rolled onto the table. In a childlike voice
the comely phantom took up the rueful lament, a stochastic suite
of unfamiliar sounds that tickled the closed ear of the tiddlywinks player and obtained in reply only an irritated wave of the
hand. *Tsk tsk, get behind me Lucifer.* The white cat outside leapt
back, scampered to the other end of the lawn. The ghostly swarm
dispersed in a tumult unheeded by the seamstress, who was working out a knot of thread, and by Gorgeous Gams, who yawned,
tired of those idiotic tiddlywinks. *Tsk tsk, get behind me Lucifer.*
Lady Jackal showed her muzzle, its wide grin of triumph floating
above the tangle of threads and winding around the tart-scented
hands, which were busy putting the buttons back into the sewing
box one by one. The thin lips in the air mouthed opaque words
that bared her teeth, eager to draw a tear of blood from the drowsy
eyes of the beautiful player who stretched with a sigh of boredom, and to bite into the heart of the seamstress who had dropped
the tangle and was holding her stomach, wincing in pain. The
opaque words, with their vacillating upstrokes, descenders leaning over the abyss, accents like teardrops hanging from eyelashes,
loops like a mouth gaping in affliction, advanced on the luminous
thread stretched between the seamstress and the somnolent
beauty. But the syllables remained mute, the message obscure,
and Lady Jackal's thin lips stretched into a different smile of triumph, the smile she used to make when she ground spices in the
mortar while relating the immemorial heartache of the witches
weeping over their human twin, loved and lost in a single night.
Their tears ran down their cheeks, then along their chest, pearled

at the tips of their breasts, fell onto their still-incandescent hearts. The lovesick witches were banished from the tribe, condemned to wander among mortals and live as pariahs, nursing the memory of their hand that died on the heart of their human twin. They understood the language of ghosts and the tingling in their stumps warned them of disaster, but it was no longer in their power to hasten its movement or divert its course. Lady Jackal laughed at those fallen sorceresses, with their widowed knowledge and their lightning premonitions that struck no one. They lagged about, madonnas of the ruins, devoured by jealousy toward the nectar gatherers, the coy seductresses, the offspring pumpers, spinners of adventure, causers of heartbreak, cutters to the quick. They lagged about, the shadow-spawn, zealously devouring their heart that was *bitter, bitter,* but they loved that, because it was their heart and because it was bitter. *Tsk, tsk, this is what love does to dreamers,* Lady Jackal had said, her eyes tearing up over the spices she crushed at the bottom of the mortar. *Tsk, tsk,* went the thin lips, pinned to the seamstress's left shoulder and crowned by a pair of eyes that sparkled with joy over the new rings from the telephone, shrieks from the darkness in which the rest of the house was plunged. Around the lamp, the seamstress was spooling the thread she had finally untangled. The beautiful player contemplated her hands that the light reflected in the gleaming table, now rid of those idiotic tiddlywinks. The thin lips flew off the seamstress's shoulder and came to rest on the last page of the book open in front of me. (*The shears of Fate have cut the tent ropes of his life, And the broker of Hope has sold him for nothing.*) The ants had started nibbling again at the tip of my already enflamed stump, which I rubbed gently on the book's deckle edge. In the middle of the page, the thin lips, hanging by their corners from the hemistiches, counted the telephone's rings with an impatient rictus. I slammed the book shut with a bang, but the thin lips had already flown off again. A sinister laugh rose from the pages, spread through the gleaming kitchen, whirled around the seamstress, who heard only the exasperating plaints of the telephone. The beautiful player smoothed her hair, mindless of the shrieks coming from the other room as of the lugubrious laugh that cascaded down and again formed their opaque words in thin air, their fine upstrokes and downstrokes bristling with thorny accents, their beautiful loops like a ribbon around a bomb. The bomb was ticking in the dark. Beneath the lamp, the roundness of the opaque words brandished the message that awaited only a hand to break the seal, untie the ribbon, pick up the telephone. But the caryatids remained unmoved, one before her well-ordered box, the other before her closed book, the third before the void, deaf to the clapper clamoring for an audience and to the crunch of tires on the gravel that signaled the meditator's return. The thin lips, releasing one last burst of lugubrious laughter, flew away from the three figurines, dove into the shrieking blackness of the dining room, and hid in the folds of the somber curtains, awaiting the entrance of the meditator, who, disconcerted by the shrinelike stillness and stumbling in the dark, rushed toward the phone to silence those slaughterhouse screams, which yielded to a metallic voice reciting a telegram from Saigon.

King Lear had left at daybreak on his bike that stayed in place. A storm had broken out overnight and a warm downpour battered the flowers in the garden, which bent low, their faces to the ground. The rain leaked through the roof, dripped on the table, formed a puddle in the middle of the anthology that for days had been open to the same page. *I shall go by the forest, I shall go by the mountain.* King Lear was in full lyrical flight. *I can remain far from you no longer.* The spool of his reveries broke in half, the actor in the rumpled suit fell flat on his face, hand clutching the shirt reddened by a hole in his heart. The cigarette dropped from his lips, his rolling eyes called for help, but the Great Deaf-Mute didn't like movies with unhappy endings and had left early. The actor in the bloodstained suit stumbled off to collapse in the gutter.

King Lear on his diabolical contraption flew like lightning, tracing garlands of fire in the sky. The Wheezer had been awakened in the middle of the night by rumblings of thunder, melded in his half-sleep with the drumbeats announcing the public beheading of the rebel poet at the Imperial Court of Hue, which he had been rereading just before bed. *Three beats of the drum and so the bitch of fate was served, A stroke of the sword and so the whore of life was gone.* The Wheezer had awakened with a start, hands outstretched to catch the poet's head. But his hands caught only the bright lozenge poking through the inky square in his window frame. The Wheezer got up, feeling around him, his legs wobbly—the Great Deaf-Mute was up to more perverse tricks, he'd bet on it. He could feel it in the weight crushing his chest, a slab virgin of inscriptions but pregnant with dangers, black with premonitions. It was still dark in his room. The storm hammered on the roof. The Wheezer went out bareheaded in the rain, crossed the slippery courtyard, entered the church by the back door, and collapsed on a chair in the front row, his eyes vacant. The slab still weighed on his chest. He could feel his bones cracking, his breath running short. He opened his mouth to pray, but only a long wail emerged, an animal scream that echoed through the darkened chamber. Screaming, he rose, kicked over the chairs, ripped apart the prayer books, threw himself at the altar, broke all the trinkets, sent the altarpiece crashing down, then touched it with a bundle of matches gathered by a hand that trembled with rage. The fire licked the weeping face of the Madonna, tickled the bloodstained feet of the Crucified One; and the varnish, peeling off, revealed the former top layer of the altarpiece, a portrait of Uncle Ho, with worm-eaten goatee, blackened eye sockets, and lips pale with fury. With a single flame the fire consumed the two messiahs, the goatee and the crown of thorns, the cross and the sickle. Screaming, shouting, fanning the blaze that spread along the electrical wires and flared between the pillars, the Wheezer rushed down from the altar and stacked the chairs from the front rows into a pyre, sprinkled with wine and quickly ignited, while above the vault the Great Deaf-Mute orchestrated a new drumroll, *And so the bitch of fate was served.* King Lear left at the sound of the drums on his wheelless, chainless cycle, which rose, light as a bubble blown through a straw, toward the blue vellum, where the Great Deaf-Mute wasn't waiting for anyone, and certainly not the Lear-bird who gripped his perch as it flew upward, while the trumpets sounded and the drums rolled. The bike rose to Heaven, *I can remain far from you no longer,* lit by garlands of fire, in a crash of thunder that made the shop signs of Saigon tremble. The little dragon, surprised in its sleep, lay low in the back of its drenched streets, indifferent to the smoke rising from the church in which a breathless Samson ransacked the lair of the Great Deaf-Mute, whining against the treacherous death that had come in the night to rob him of his strength and steal his friend's companionship, spirit him away on his diabolical contraption up a ray of light that stretched across the vellum, now cleansed of its fiery garlands and restored to its azure blue. In the church, the pyre of chairs gave off acrid smoke, and Samson, half blinded, railing like one moribund, added to it whatever he could lay his hands on—devotional trinkets, flowers from the altar, prayer books—sparing only the scrap of swaddling in its bell jar. Day was breaking over Saigon. The actor in the rumpled suit managed to blurt out *son of a bitch!* But the bitch of fate had bid her farewell, leaving him to croak in the gutter, mouth hanging open, a hole in his heart. King Lear, on his cycle that was forging its way through the heights, smiled to see his princesses' favorite actor with his head against the curb, his suit in the filthy water. The velocipede volplaned toward the blue vellum like a vagabond skiff in the zephyr that the evanescent ire of the Great Veteran had vented to revive the city's pavilions, ravaged by the violent squalls of the eve. The lookout vaulted on his yardarm, nose to the wind, twenty thousand leagues over the vociferous streets and the comings and goings of the vibrios who demivolted without lifting their eyes toward the flying fool on his fast vehicle navigating between the white veils. The late King Lear was making his great voyage toward the blue vellum, while in the city the tousled vibrios straddled vrooming little dragons that flew from the alleys and flowed toward the boulevards, where the flood of flivvers honked in a flux and reflux. The high-flying bird hovered over the metropolis, marveling at the cranes that from this distance looked like compasses, and the villas, whiter than new erasers, lining avenues straight as rulers, near covered markets that looked like cricket boxes and made him feel like dipping his hand and lifting the lid. Farther on, the black muddy river flowed like the ink spilled long ago, so long ago, by his two squabbling little princesses. The ink had spilled the length of the table (the one on which King Lear, in his exit, had left the open volume of poems) and the squabblers had stood there, petrified at seeing the wood drink up the dark trail. Then tears, flowing abundantly down their cheeks, had gone to mix with the black river that cut the table in half. King Lear, his hands on their penitent little heads, had improvised a story about a city divided by a river as black as the ink that soaked into the wood of the table and stained the squabblers' elbows. In this city lived two lovers, a prince and a princess, who were separated by the river. Once a bridge had joined the two banks, but the last war had ended with the building of a wall that blocked the bridge and rose high into the sky. The prince and the princess met at the edge of the water and gazed at each other, while the river flowed impassibly between them. Then the prince fell ill. Knowing he was doomed, he slid a few lines, *I can remain far from you no longer*, in a hollow reed, which he sent over the river currents toward the princess. The next day, the currents brought him in the same reed a lament that ended with the word *Come*. The prince built a boat that he pushed toward the water. But the stakes planted in the riverbed after the last war sunk the fragile craft. The prince returned home, shaking with fever. He was too weak to scale the wall, but that night he dreamed he was leaning on a long perch that would send him vaulting over it in a miraculous leap. On waking, he asked for large rolls of drawing paper to sketch out the design of a giant kite. He wanted to make himself wings, great shimmering wings that would carry him to the far side of the bridge. He applied himself to his task, despite fever and exhaustion. He even forgot about the meetings at river's edge, where the princess waited for him, weeping with anxiety. She wept so many, many tears that the river swelled and overflowed its banks. When finally the prince took flight, rose into the sky while beating his wings, he saw from above only the inundated banks, the engulfed palace, and bodies floating in the black water. Then he ceased beating his wings and the variegated bird, spinning around and around, let itself fall into the black river, where his silt-covered wings formed a bridge to span the two banks. The shadow of the flying fool on his fast vehicle danced on the blue partition like a mirage drawn by white volutes. King Lear pursued his journey, accompanied by the brouhaha of the city that rose as the storm receded. Amid the morning rumble of construction sites, the fanfare of a brass band broke out, covering the aubade of itinerant hawkers and the hurly-burly of the first car horns. The mournful sound of a trumpet unleashed a cacophony of horns. The Last Judgment marching band roused the city, which watched as horn players and drummers, all dressed in white, kept time with the buglers who raised their instruments at each signal from the master of ceremonies—who, gloved in white, coiffed in an immaculate helmet, directed the choreography of the six pallbearers squeezed into their white uniforms, marching in cadence while shouldering the leaden casket. Behind them came a procession of tearful silhouettes veiled in white, but the brass band drowned out the sobs of the hired mourners, and King Lear on his cycle only had eyes for the tail of the cortege, a cluster of little girls in white who twirled around, pinched each others' waists, jabbed each other with their elbows, hopped up and down impatiently, repressed their giggles, and twisted between their fingers the ends of the long mourning ribbons that encircled their tiny heads. Zigzagging like a dragon whose head spat the flames of hell while its tail wagged carelessly, the procession headed toward the church to the rhythm of this apocalyptic hullabaloo, which exasperated the mourners in their noisy dolor and made the little girls bubble over with laughter. The doors of the church were shut; rubberneckers congregated around the lair of the Great Deaf-Mute, which gave off billows of acrid smoke. From within came a sound of bellowing, a great crashing din, followed by a long silence. Then the portal creaked and the wings opened onto the dark abode, littered with debris and staved-in chairs. At the back, a pyre was crackling. The Wheezer, his great shadow looming behind him, rushed forward in his black, ash-stained robe and, shoving through the brass band that had fallen silent in stupor, ran off as fast as his legs would carry him, flew across the road, and dove into an alley where his tall silhouette was swallowed by the crowd. *And so the bitch of fate was served.*